ONE

There was something natural and unassuming about Matt, something so likeable and endearing that it would be hard not to love him, given half a chance.

Did his twin, Brad, have the same qualities? I wondered. There were differences between them, yes. I had already noted that. Matt was more outgoing. But beneath his reserve, was Brad just as exciting as Matt? It was an intriguing question.

What had started out as a routine, boring summer was turning into the most interesting one of my life.

Bantam Sweet Dreams Romances
Ask your bookseller for the books you have missed

One Boy Too Many

Marian Caudell

BANTAM BOOKS

TORONTO · NEW YORK · LONDON · SYDNEY · AUCKLAND

RL 6, IL age 11 and up

ONE BOY TOO MANY
A Bantam Book / January 1986

Cover photo by Pat Hill

ISBN 0-553-25297-6

Published simultaneously in the United States and Canada

*Bantam Books are published by Bantam Books, Inc. Its trademark,
consisting of the words "Bantam Books" and the portrayal of a
rooster, is registered in U.S. Patent and Trademark Office and in
other countries. Marca Registrada. Bantam Books, Inc., 666 Fifth
Avenue, New York, New York 10103.*

Printed and bound in Great Britain by Hunt Barnard Printing Ltd.

O   0 9 8 7 6 5 4 3 2 1

One Boy Too Many

Chapter One

"Not now, Baffin," I said absently. "Go away."

Baffin, our black Labrador, ignored my plea and nudged my neck with his nose. His whiskers tickled.

I laughed and leaned away from him. "I'm reading, Baffin. Just let me finish this book, and then I'll take you for a walk. I'm almost done." I settled a little deeper into the blue overstuffed armchair, my favorite place to read.

Baffin gave up on my neck, and whining softly, he flopped his head down in my lap. I glanced below my paperback, *Love at Summer Camp*, and saw a pair of liquid brown eyes regarding me with a mixture of eagerness, love, and accusation.

1

It was more than I could stand. "Oh, all right," I said, reluctantly laying my book down on the coffee table. "I'll finish it later."

Baffin trotted to the front door and sniffed impatiently while I went to the closet and got his leash. The leash is strictly for appearance sake. Baffin weighs almost as much as I do, ninety-five pounds to my one hundred, but he's a lot stronger than I am. He could get away from me anytime.

"I'm taking Baffin for a walk, Mom," I called as I snapped the leash onto his collar. "Be back in a few minutes."

Mom's voice came from the back of the house, raised above the sound of the TV. "All right, but you'd better hurry. It's already seven-thirty."

I hadn't realized it was that late. No wonder Baffin was impatient. I usually took him out before seven, but I was so wrapped up in my book that I'd lost all track of time. I do that a lot when I'm reading, especially if it's a romance novel. I love romances—young adult romances, that is. I like to imagine that I'm the heroine and all the exciting things in the book are happening to me. But so far none of them had.

Oh, I'd had some dates, like most sixteen-year-old girls, but none of them had made me feel the way the characters in my books did—exciting, desirable, sophisticated, grown-up. They had their share of problems, too, but they always managed to solve them by the end of the book. Well, I thought, opening the screen door, the only problem I had right then was Baffin, and he wasn't really a problem.

"Lead the way," I said as we started down the steps. I hooked one finger through the loop on Baffin's leash, letting it dangle loosely between us. Baffin usually didn't lunge at anything, but if he did, I didn't want to be dragged along behind.

"The girls will think we've forgotten them, Baffin," I said, quickening my step.

Tina and Anne Carlton were my charges for the summer. I sat with them from eleven to four every weekday while their mother, a teacher, commuted to the university to work on her master's. This was the third summer I'd done it, and I'd grown very fond of them. They were almost like little sisters to me.

The girls loved Baffin, and I took him over some evenings to see them. I couldn't take him with me when I went over to sit because Mrs. Carlton didn't like dogs in the house and I couldn't stand to see him tied up outside. Besides, I took Tina and Anne to the pool every day, and I sure couldn't take Baffin there!

Baffin was just as crazy about the girls as they were about him. He was so used to our nightly routine that he headed straight for their house, five blocks away. We were strolling along at our usual pace when Baffin suddenly stopped, raised his head, and sniffed.

"What is it, boy?" I asked. I didn't smell anything, but then his sense of smell was much better than mine.

Instead of crossing the street, Baffin turned the corner and began to trot. I had to run to keep up with him. I didn't see anything ahead except a red car parked in front of the old Emery place, which had been vacant for a year.

As we neared the car, the front door on the driver's side opened. Out climbed a guy I had never seen before. He was carrying a small white sack in his hand.

Baffin came to an abrupt halt next to the car, and I followed close behind.

"Who's taking whom for a walk?" the boy asked, his bright blue eyes alive with amusement.

"I thought I was taking him, but I'm not so sure about that last half block," I answered with a nervous laugh. He was the cutest boy I had ever seen, with hair the color of corn silk. Then I looked from him to the house and

4

noticed crisp, white curtains covering the windows. "Do you live here?" I asked, disbelief in my voice.

"Yes. Why? Is there something wrong with the house? Is it haunted?"

"N-n-no," I stammered. "I was just surprised. I didn't know anyone had moved in."

Baffin began to prance, and I said under my breath, "Sit, Baffin." Baffin sat on his haunches, and I put my hand on his head, which was almost level with my waist. I could feel him quivering. A sound came from his throat, a cross between a growl and a sob.

"Does he bite?" asked the boy, taking a cautious step backward.

"No." I smiled. "He's as gentle as a kitten."

"I'll take your word for it, but I still don't like the way he's looking at me. Are you sure he wouldn't like to take a bit out of me?"

Only then did I notice that the sack he was holding was from McDonald's. I could smell the french fries in it. I had been too preoccupied to notice before.

"It's not you he's after," I explained, hoping I appeared more composed than I felt. "It's your fries. He loves fries. He can smell them a mile away."

"In that case, I think I'd better give him one before he decides that I look better than they do." Reaching into the bag, he picked up a couple of fries and tossed them at Baffin's feet.

Baffin dropped his head, scooped up the fries, and sat up for more, eyeing the sack greedily. The boy threw him another one.

"Have you lived here long?" I asked.

"A week," he answered, tossing yet another fry out. "Just for insurance," he added with a smile so warm and friendly that it almost took my breath away.

A week, I thought. How could I have missed such a good-looking guy living right in my own neighborhood?

"My dad is with Shuster Electronics," he continued. "Last month he got transferred from Ohio—" A loud bang sounded from the direction of the house, and the boy interrupted himself with, "Sorry, got to go."

He raced up the steps and opened the screen door. Then he turned around and asked, "You live around here?"

"Yes. Down there around the corner." I gestured with my right hand.

"Good. See you later then." He disappeared, letting the screen door slam shut behind him.

Baffin, his mission accomplished, turned around and started back to the corner. I followed him in a bit of a daze; the boy's last words had filled me with happy anticipation.

As we approached the two-story colonial, I saw that Tina and Anne were sitting on the front steps waiting for us. With their identical soft red curls and freckles, they could almost pass for twins, especially at a distance. I had to smile at how cute they looked, each forlornly holding her chin in her hands.

"What kept you?" asked Anne when Baffin and I reached her. "I thought you weren't coming." Anne was the ten-year-old, and she was more aggressive than eight-year-old Tina, who threw her arms around Baffin's neck and gave him a hug.

"I was reading," I admitted. "And lost track of the time."

"You're always reading," said Tina as she gently stroked Baffin's fur. "Don't you ever do anything else?"

I daydream, I thought, *about boys like the one I just met*. I didn't say so, though. Instead I said, "Sure I do. I take you swimming every day, don't I?"

"Yeah," Tina went on. "But you don't swim much. You just lie around and read. I get enough reading at school to last me all summer."

I sat down beside Anne, and Baffin worked his way between the girls so that each one had an arm around his neck. Baffin was in heaven. He liked to be fussed over almost as much as he liked fries.

Anne, who had been unusually quiet, was watching me and frowning. "What's wrong?" she asked.

"Nothing," I said. "Why?"

"You look kind of funny, kind of—of—far away. Like you're not really here."

Tina stopped petting Baffin long enough to glance in my direction. "She looks OK to me."

Anne rolled her eyes up and sighed as if to say that Tina was too young to understand such things. She leaned over and whispered in my ear, "Is it a boy?"

"No-o-o," I whispered back, shaking my head from side to side and smiling at her. "It's just your imagination." I stood up, held my arms out, and turned around. "See? I look just the same as I always do."

"I told you there wasn't anything wrong with her," said Tina triumphantly.

Anne dropped the subject, much to my relief, and we spent the next half an hour or so just playing with Baffin.

On the way home I glanced down the

street where the boy lived. There were lights on in his house, and the red car was still parked outside, but there was no one in sight. I have to say that I was kind of disappointed.

My house was quiet when we got home. Mom left me a note that she and Dad had gone shopping. So after I had hung up Baffin's leash, I picked up my book, settled comfortably in my armchair, and began reading again. I could still picture myself as the heroine, but I had a little trouble with the hero. Instead of seeing him as he was described in the book, with dark hair and dark eyes, I was seeing him with corn silk hair, blue eyes, and a smile that could melt a heart.

Chapter Two

At first I thought it was a distant alarm ringing. But when I realized it was the phone, I snuggled back down under the covers and tried to recapture the romantic dream I had been having. A dark-eyed stranger was bending down to kiss me when Mom called up to me. The dream fell apart.

"Jenny, it's Mrs. Carlton," she called. I hoped our upstairs phone would be fixed soon, so I wouldn't have to go all the way downstairs to talk.

With a loud groan and a sleepy OK I climbed out of bed, slipped a robe on over my nightshirt, and padded downstairs to the kitchen, wondering what Mrs. Carlton had run out of this time.

"Hello, Mrs. Carlton," I said, picking up the phone.

"Oh, Jenny," said Mrs. Carlton a little breathlessly, "do you mind?"

I didn't have to ask her what she meant. Two or three times a week Mrs. Carlton would run out of something and ask me to pick it up on my way over. "Of course not," I replied. "What are we out of?"

"Milk. I used the last we had for breakfast, and I'm running late or I'd pick it up myself."

"I'll get some on the way over," I told her. "A gallon of two percent, right?"

"Yes, and thanks."

I heard her sigh of relief before she hung up. It wasn't very far to the market, but it was out of the way, which meant I'd have to hurry. Pouring myself a glass of milk, I picked up a doughnut and carried them both up to my room where I ate as I dressed.

Ordinarily I wore my swimsuit with a pair of shorts over it to the Carltons' so I wouldn't have to change after I got there, but since I was going to the market first, I put on a shirt, too.

When I was ready to go—a towel, some baby oil, and a new paperback stuffed into my tote bag—I looked around to say goodbye to

Mom. Then I heard her in the basement doing the laundry. I called down the stairs, "I'm leaving. I'll have the car back a little after four."

Mom peered up at me with a stack of towels in her hands. "No hurry, dear. I took your father to work this morning, so I have his."

I had hoped I'd get my own car when I turned sixteen, but Dad said two cars were enough for a family of three, and so far it had worked out all right. Mom let me use hers when I baby-sat so I could take the girls out, and she was very generous with it in the evenings, too.

I decided to turn a couple of blocks before I usually did, so I could drive by the house where I had seen the blond boy. Of course he wasn't there, but I couldn't help wondering where he was and what he was doing.

I parked as close as I could to the entrance of the market and then hurried by the fruit and vegetable section to the aisle with the dairy counter. Picking up a gallon of milk, I turned around and caught my breath. Heading straight toward me was the boy with corn silk hair. I couldn't see his eyes because he was looking down at the shelves, but I knew they were blue. He was just as cute as I'd remembered. When he got closer, I said, "Hi!"

At first I thought he hadn't heard me, but then he looked up.

"Hi," I said again, smiling.

"Hello," he said rather uncertainly, as if he weren't sure I was really talking to him.

"Can I help you find something?" I asked brightly. "I know where just about everything is."

He hesitated and then shook his head slightly. "I've found almost everything I need. But thanks." His tone was very formal, and the expression in his eyes was reserved and a little distant. I wondered what had happened to make the sparkle of the night before go out of them.

Then it hit me. He didn't recognize me, didn't even remember our talk. It was more than a little disconcerting. He had been in my thoughts so much that I had taken for granted I had been in his. Or at least that he wouldn't have forgotten me so quickly.

Feeling somewhat foolish, I mumbled, "It's OK," and made my way to the checkout counter. Had I only imagined the "See you later" when he'd rushed into the house as Bafflin and I stood on the sidewalk?

I was feeling pretty disappointed by the time I got to the Carltons', but I tried to hide it.

Mrs. Carlton was waiting for me on the front porch. "Thanks so much, Jenny," she said. "You're a lifesaver. I don't know what we'd do without you."

"It's OK, Mrs. Carlton," I replied. "The girls inside?"

"Yes. They've already got their swimsuits on."

I waved goodbye as she backed out of the drive and then let myself into the house.

The girls were eager to go, so we piled their towels, lotion, and toys into the car and took off. We got to the pool just after it opened, so I got my favorite spot, right at the edge and about halfway between the shallow end and the diving end. The girls are pretty good swimmers. Most of the time they stay in the shallow water, but occasionally they wander into the deep end. Halfway between is the best place to keep an eye on them.

I went in with them for a half hour or so and then climbed out and began to rub some oil on my arms and legs. Anne swam over and looked up at me.

"You're so brown you don't need any tanning lotion," she said wistfully. She was leaning out of the water with her arms resting on the concrete edge.

"It's not tanning lotion," I told her. "It's oil—to keep my skin from drying out. But I think you could use some sunscreen. Hang on a minute."

I walked over to her and crouched down so I could rub the lotion on her shoulders. "You're getting red."

"I always get red," Anne complained. "Never brown, like you. I wish I looked like you. You're not only tan, you're pretty, too."

"Why, Anne," I said, "so are you. I'd love to have curly hair like yours instead of this straight mop." I lifted my long, black hair off my neck and let it fall down my back.

"You can always curl it or get a permanent."

"Never mind," I said. "One day you're going to be very beautiful." And I was sure she would be. I wondered if I had been that concerned about my looks when I was her age. I couldn't remember, but I thought that I probably had been.

Anne swam away, and I stretched out on my stomach, facing the pool, and picked up my paperback, *Always in Love*. Sometimes I met some of my friends at the pool, but I didn't see any of them around, so I was thankful I'd brought the book.

The heroine, Marcie Davenport, was a girl my age. She had just moved from the country to a large city and was pretty lonely for the first few days. Then she met Allen, who seemed to be a clean-cut, all-American, ideal boy. He was cute, tall, dark, intelligent, considerate. What more could she ask for?

I looked up from the book to check on the girls, then let my mind wander. I liked the description of Allen and the way he treated Marcie, taking her to shows, dances, and plays, always attentive and charming. But there was another character in the book, one that I felt sure was going to play a major role in Marcie's life.

She had met him on the first day of school. He was her lab partner in Chemistry II, and she had liked him instantly, sensing that they had a lot in common. But before she had a chance to really find out, Allen overwhelmed her with his attentions, and the other boy, Cary, sort of faded into the background, as far as she was concerned, except during chem class.

I had the feeling that in the end, Marcie would come to realize that, while she had a lot of fun with Allen, their relationship was only superficial and what she really wanted was someone she could talk to, someone who was comfortable to be with, someone who shared her own interests and concerns, someone like Cary.

I sighed and went back to my book. I was so absorbed in it that when a shadow fell over the page, I thought the sun had gone behind a cloud. Then I heard someone say, "Hi."

"Hi," I said automatically, glancing up from the book and expecting to see one of my friends. Then my eyes widened behind my sunglasses, and I sat up, closing the book and laying it facedown beside me. It was the blond boy.

"I was hoping I might find you here," he said, swinging himself up onto the pool deck so that he sat beside me. He looked over my shoulder before he leaned close and whispered, "You didn't bring your dog, did you?"

"No." I laughed and added, "They don't allow dogs at the pool."

"Good," he said, grinning mischievously. "It's not that I don't like dogs, you know. It's just—" He lifted his hand from the pool deck to indicate Baffin's size and shuddered in mock terror.

I was glad he couldn't see the confusion in my eyes. He had been so friendly the night before but so distant that morning. Now he was being not only friendly, but charming as well. I hoped he wasn't one of those moody people who swung from high to low without warning, but that was the only way to explain the change in him.

"I didn't see you come in," I said.

"You were too engrossed in your book," he replied. "What are you reading?"

"Just a novel. Nothing important." Most boys aren't interested in romance novels. "Did you have enough fries left last night to go around?"

"Just barely." His smile sent goose bumps down my spine. I liked him much better this way than the way he'd been that morning. "But Brad and I are used to sharing."

"Brad?"

"M-m-hm-m. My brother." He glanced toward the diving board, and I followed his gaze. Then I gasped involuntarily and looked again from him to the boy on the high dive.

"You're twins!" I exclaimed. "Identical twins!"

"Not identical," said the boy. "We just look alike."

No wonder the boy in the supermarket had been so hesitant. He'd never seen me before. He must have thought I was terribly forward. My face began to burn at the thought, and I added hastily, "I ran into your twin in the market this morning, but I thought he was you."

"And I'll bet you wondered why he didn't recognize you."

"Yes," I said, still embarrassed.

"It happens all the time," he said. "Until people get to know us, that is. Then we're easy to tell apart. I'm the one who does all the talking. Brad's the quiet one. I'm Matt. Matt Hunter. I should have introduced myself last night."

"Jenny," I said, smiling. "Jenny Warner."

"Hello, Jenny Warner. That's a pretty name. Jenny."

"Matt's a nice name, too," I said. "Short for Matthew?"

"Uh-huh. Jenny short for Jennifer?"

"No. I'm just plain Jenny." Out of the corner of my eye I could see Anne standing very still in the pool and watching us.

"Jenny, but definitely not plain." He smiled at me again in a way that made me feel weak.

"Are you in the phone book, Jenny?"

"Yes," I said. "Under Howard, Howard Warner, that is."

"Then I'll see you later."

He slipped into the water, and I watched as he swam toward the deep end where his twin, Brad, was waiting at the foot of the high dive. I had forgotten all about Anne until she swam over to the side of the pool and asked softly, "It was a boy, wasn't it?"

"What do you mean?" I asked, pretending ignorance.

"Last night. That's why you looked so funny. You were thinking about him. Who is he?"

"A new boy in town." I tried to shrug it off. Anne turned around to watch Matt swim the length of the pool.

When he climbed out of the water and joined his brother, she exclaimed, "Wow! There are two of him!"

And both are cute, I thought, *but why wouldn't they be? They're twins. Identical twins.* Not identical in personality, according to Matt. I knew there must be other differences between them. I wondered what they were.

My book forgotten, I watched the two boys as they practiced various dives. I found that by adjusting my sunglasses I could look out of the corner of my eye without appearing to be looking straight at them.

Right away I noticed some differences.

Brad was very serious about his form on the high dive. He would space his feet just so, take a deep breath, hold it for just a second, and then spring. He cut the water like a knife. Matt's dives were not quite so precise. They were very good, but he tended to splash a little more when he entered the water. Occasionally one would turn to the other and say something. I couldn't hear what they said, but I had no trouble telling them apart. Matt's reply would usually be accompanied with a bright smile and Brad's with a smile that was more reserved.

I was too far away to notice any small differences in their facial features, but Matt was a little more athletic looking.

"I don't blame you for being entranced," said a voice beside me.

I jumped slightly. "Jody! You startled me."

"I've been sitting right here next to you for the last five minutes," she told me. It was Jody Wininger, one of my close friends.

"Oh," I said with a guilty start. "I didn't see you come in."

"Obviously," said Jody dryly. Her freckled nose wrinkled in merriment, and her blue eyes danced. "Who are they?"

There was no use pretending I didn't

know what she was talking about. She had been watching me watch them long enough to know better.

"New boys in town," I replied, trying to sound offhanded. "Matt and Brad Hunter."

"You've met them already?"

"Just barely." I told Jody my experiences with the twins. "So, you see," I wound up. "I don't really know either one."

"But you'd like to," insisted Jody, giving me a knowing smile.

I grinned back at her but didn't admit anything. I didn't have to. Jody knew me too well.

"Want to bet one of them calls you before the week is out?" asked Jody.

I didn't take the bet. Partly because Matt had implied that he would call me and partly because I didn't want to bet against something I wanted to happen.

"Interesting," mused Jody, turning her gaze back to the boys. "Almost makes me sorry I'm with Bill."

"Almost, but not quite," I said with certainty. Jody and Bill had been an item for three years, and they were devoted to each other. In fact, it wasn't often that I had a chance to be alone with Jody, to talk girl talk, and I was enjoying it.

And she was right. It was an interesting situation, one that made me sure that something new and different and wonderful was about to begin.

Chapter Three

Mom and Dad went out to play cards with some friends that night, so I had the house all to myself. Ours is an old house in an old tree-lined section of town. It was built sometime around the turn of the century; the rooms are all big with high ceilings. When we'd moved in ten years before, Dad converted the dining room into a TV room. The former living room became a dining room, and the "parlor" at the front of the house, at one time used only for Sunday visitors, became our living room. It was a nice arrangement. If the TV was on, it didn't distract anyone in the front of the house.

I didn't feel like watching TV, so I sat in the living room and picked up *Always in Love. . . .*

* * *

Marcie and Allen had become one of the most popular couples in school. They were invited to every event and they spent so much time together that Marcie was beginning to worry about her grades. But whenever she brought up the subject of studying, Allen would look down at her, raise his eyebrows, and give her his crooked, fetching, are-you-kidding grin. Her heart would skip a beat, and she would rationalize her worries away.

I was enjoying the things Marcie and Allen did together and was thinking how exciting Marcie's life was, but I was also worried about Cary. It was clear to me, if not to Marcie, that he was in love with her. There was much more to Cary than Marcie realized, and I hoped she would find out before it was too late.

I was tempted to skip ahead through the book, reading a line here and there, just to find out if Cary would eventually let Marcie know how he felt about her, but I didn't.

I was feeling sorry for Cary when Baffin came over and put his head in my lap. "I don't want to go out now, Baffin," I said.

He sat up and began to nuzzle my neck again.

"How about going out in the backyard?" I asked, laying my book down.

He understood that and trotted toward

the back of the house. When I opened the door for him, he went outside, then stopped and looked back at me, waiting for me to follow him.

"I'm not coming out right now," I told him. "Maybe later."

Baffin continued to sit staring at the door even after I closed it. I watched through the kitchen window, feeling guilty because I knew he wanted company and that that wasn't too much to ask.

When a bell sounded, I snatched up the phone, which was next to me.

"Hello."

There was nothing but a dial tone. I felt very foolish when I realized it was the door bell and not the phone.

Wondering who it could be, I hurried to the front door, opened it, and gasped with surprise and delight. Matt was standing there, holding a carton of french fries and grinning mischievously.

"What—" I began.

He held a finger to his lips and looked over my shoulder.

"He's in the backyard," I whispered, knowing instantly who he was looking for.

Matt sighed in mock relief, grinned again,

and said, "Confucius say, 'Never call on pretty girl without french fries for dog.' "

I stifled a giggle. "I doubt if Confucius ever heard of french fries."

He frowned. "Really?"

"Really."

"Well, maybe it was fortune cookies then. But they didn't have any fortune cookies at McDonald's, so he'll have to settle for these."

"He'll love them, and you, too, for bringing them. Come on in." I'd had other surprise visits from boys but never one with an approach like Matt's.

I led him through to the back of the house. As soon as Baffin heard our footsteps, he ran up to the door and began to bark excitedly. I finally opened it and we got out. When Baffin saw Matt and the fries, he pranced and barked some more.

"Over here, Baffin," I said. "By the picnic table."

Matt and I sat on the same side with our backs to the tabletop. Baffin sat in front of us, his tail wagging impatiently, looking from Matt to me to the fries. Then he concentrated on the fries.

"Do I give them to him all at once?" asked Matt.

"You can," I said. "But he prefers to be hand fed."

"After you," offered Matt, holding the carton out.

I picked up a fry and held it out by the tip. Baffin gulped it down after one quick bite. Then I took another and just let it lie in the palm of my hand. Baffin took that one, too.

"See?" I said. "There's nothing to it."

It was Matt's turn. He hesitantly offered Baffin a fry but then let him eat out of his hand. Baffin saw who had control of the fries, so he moved closer to Matt.

About halfway through the fries, Matt put a hand on Baffin's head and stroked his fur. "He's beautiful."

Our conversation had been very easy and relaxed as long as we had Baffin and the fries to talk about. But when Matt looked at me, I felt a lump begin to rise in my throat. I hadn't felt tongue-tied at the pool, but there were a lot of people around us, a lot of noise. It was all very impersonal there. Now we were alone and it was very quiet and very personal.

"What have you been doing since you got to town?" I asked inanely.

"Looking for a job, mostly," replied Matt. "But I haven't had much luck so far. It's awfully hard to find work at the beginning of

August. We picked a poor time to move. Poor for job hunting, anyhow. And my parents are the old-fashioned type. They expect us to earn our spending money."

"So do mine," I said. "I baby-sit during the day. It doesn't pay a whole lot, but it helps." I made a mental note to hold down expenses and suggest going dutch if Matt asked me out.

"How about your brother? Has he found any work?" I asked.

"No, not yet. What we'd like is full-time work now and part-time when school starts. We both have applications in at all the factories, and we've tried the big resort hotel, too. You've been there." It was a statement, not a question.

"Sure," I said. "Lots of times. That's where we had the junior prom last year. I helped decorate the ballroom. Next year I'll be one of the honored seniors."

Mentioning the prom must have made Matt think about dates because he asked, "Are you going with anyone?"

"No. Not now," I added. I had been dating Tom Clark, but we had broken up just before the prom. We went to it together anyway, though, because it was too late to look for other dates and we did dance well together. We had a nice time, and we were still friends.

29

Matt reached over, took my hand in his, and smiled softly at me. "Good. I'm glad you're free right now."

I felt my throat begin to tighten up, and I knew that if I didn't say something quick, I wouldn't be able to talk at all. The prom reminded me of school and of how little I knew about Matt, so I asked, "What class will you be in next year?" I knew he wasn't out of school because of what he had said about part-time work.

"We'll be seniors, also," he answered. Then he snapped his fingers and grinned. "There I go again, saying 'we' instead of 'I.' "

"You and Brad, is it?"

"Uh-huh."

"All the twins I know have names that rhyme or names that at least start with the same letter. How did your folks decide on Matt and Brad?"

"They thought there was going to be just one of us, and Mom wanted to name him after her dad, Bradley Matthew."

"So they split the name. Don't tell me," I added hastily. "Brad was born first."

"Right. He's my 'older' brother." There was a twinkle in his eye.

"You must be very close."

"We are."

"What about school activities?" I asked, hoping I didn't look as flustered as I felt. "Are you going to go out for any sports?" He was athletic-looking and tall, so I knew that Mr. Martin, the basketball coach, would be interested in him.

"I'd like to. It depends on whether I can find work and, if I do, what my hours will be. I played football back in Ohio and really enjoyed it. How about you? I'll bet you're involved in all sorts of activities."

"Not many. Tri-Hi-Y, with all its fund-raising projects for charities, keeps me pretty busy. And the only other school organization I belong to is Pep Club. We don't do much except sit together and cheer for our team at the games."

"Any plans for after next year?"

"I'll go to college somewhere," I replied. "But I haven't decided where yet. You?"

"Same here. There are so many things I'd like to do that I can't make up my mind."

I was about to ask him what some of those things were, but he stood up and said, "I'd better be going. I didn't tell anyone where I'd be."

"I'm glad you came over," I said simply.

"So am I. Are you going to the pool tomorrow? I could pick you up anytime after twelve-thirty."

"I'll be there, but I have to take Tina and Anne." He looked so disappointed that I quickly explained who they were.

"Then I'll see you there," he said with a smile that sent my heart skipping again.

We talked a bit more as I led him back through the house, with Baffin following close behind.

Matt waved when he got to the sidewalk, and Baffin and I watched until he rounded the corner and was out of sight.

"Well, Baffin," I said, looking down into his upturned face, "what do you think about that?"

Baffin wagged his tail, and I leaned down and hugged him.

I got up earlier than usual the next morning so that if Mrs. Carlton needed me to go to the market, I'd still have plenty of time to decide which swimsuit to wear and how to fix my hair.

I wished I had gotten a permanent before the summer began instead of deciding to wait until just before school started, the way I'd always done. At least I hadn't had it cut. I always curl the ends under before I go to school or out on a date, but in the summer when I know I'm going swimming, curling my hair is a waste of time unless I stay out of the water. And that isn't any fun.

I stood in front of the mirror and pulled the sides of my hair back with barrettes. It didn't look very good that way, so I tried pinning it up on top of my head. That didn't look like me, so I ended up just letting it fall down my back, as usual.

Then I opened the door of my closet, whose roof line slipped under the eaves. My room is upstairs at the back of the house. It isn't large, but it has two dormer windows and a window seat that stretches between them. I love to curl up there with a good book, especially on rainy days.

I think my room must have belonged to the maid of the house years before because it's at the far end of the hall, sort of private, and has its own bath. Dad had a shower installed to replace the old square tub when we moved in. Then he built bookshelves on both sides of the door, which I filled with books, books, books.

The colorful book covers lent a splash of color to an otherwise all gold-and-white room. Mom had found an antique dressing table and painted it gold and white to match my brass bed and the deep amber carpet.

I took two swimsuits off their hangers and decided to wear the black one. There wasn't a lot of difference in the styles of the two suits, but the black one was a little more comfortable than the red one. It wasn't cut quite so high on the sides.

My preparations didn't take as long as I thought they would, and since Mrs. Carlton hadn't called, I was ready ahead of time. I figured I would go on over to the Carltons' anyway. For the first time I didn't pack a book in my tote bag.

It turned out that we got to the pool a little later than usual because Tina dropped a jar of grape jelly on the kitchen floor, and it took forever to clean up. When we finally did arrive, I had to park far away from the entrance. I could see Matt and Brad from the lot. They were sitting side by side at the deep end, dangling their feet in the pool. I couldn't tell them apart at that distance.

I wondered if I should go right over to Matt and let him know I was there. Then I decided I'd better claim my spot so I could keep a close watch on the girls. After all, my first duty was to them.

They wanted to jump right in, so I carried

their towels and mine around the shallow end to my station. As I spread my towel, I looked in Matt's direction. He saw me, waved, slipped into the water, and swam straight over.

"Hi," he said when he reached my side of the pool. "Are you alone? I thought you had to bring some little girls with you."

"I did," I replied. "They're out there." I pointed toward the shallow end of the pool. "The two redheads, Anne and Tina. Tina's the little one."

The girls hadn't noticed Matt yet, and I was glad. I'm sure Anne could have seen the stars in my eyes. So would Jody if she had been there, but I knew she was working at the mall. The day before had been her day off.

Matt asked, "Can you swim, or do you have to watch them all the time?"

"I can swim," I said and slipped into the pool beside him. "The guards are very good with kids here. But I do check on them every few minutes," I added hastily.

"Good. I want Brad to meet you."

We swam across to the diving section. Matt was a strong swimmer and made it there in only five or six strokes. I was a good swimmer, too, but it took me a little longer because my arms were shorter than his.

Brad was still sitting on the edge of the

pool when we climbed up the ladder, so Matt led me over to him. "Brad," he said, "meet Jenny Warner. Jenny, Brad."

Brad and I said hello to each other and then Matt dropped down to the concrete edge, leaving a space for me between him and Brad.

I felt a little giddy, sitting between two such cute boys, and a little self-conscious, too, as if everyone were watching me. But when I glanced up, I saw that no one was paying any attention to us.

"How do you like Spring Waters so far, Brad?" I asked.

"Just fine," he said, smiling. "What I've seen of it, that is. We've been pretty busy so far."

His smile was genuine, if not as spontaneous as Matt's. And on closer inspection, I saw that his jaw was a little squarer than his brother's. It made him look kind of rugged. There was a difference in their eyes, too, but it was hard to define. Brad's were warm and friendly, but they didn't twinkle the way Matt's did. Maybe that was just because he didn't know me very well, I thought, remembering our meeting at the market.

"I think one of your charges is waving at you," said Matt.

I shaded my eyes with my hand, and there

was Tina waving for me to come on in. "Duty calls," I said, getting to my feet. "Nice to meet you, Brad."

He smiled that same slow smile and returned the compliment. "Nice to meet you, Jenny."

Matt and I dived in side by side and swam up to Tina. "What's wrong?" I asked.

"Nothing. I just wanted you to swim with us for a while."

I introduced both girls to Matt. Tina took him at face value, but Anne studied him covertly.

"Can we go in the deep water, Jenny?" asked Tina. Sometimes, if the pool wasn't crowded, I let the girls swim across the deep end, one at a time, with me right beside them.

Before I could answer, Matt said, "How would you like to go piggyback?"

"Piggyback?" asked Tina.

"Sure. Just put your hands on my shoulders, and I'll ferry you across." Matt turned around so his back was to Tina. Then he bent his knees until his shoulders were under the water.

"Hop on," he said.

Tina, clearly delighted at so much attention, held on to Matt's shoulders as he swam across the pool, pulling her along with him.

"That was fun," she said when they returned. "You ought to try it, Jenny."

"I'm afraid I'm a little too big for that," I said, feeling the blood rush to my face at the thought of being that close to Matt.

"No, you aren't," she insisted. "It's real easy. You just float along on top of the water."

Matt grinned at me invitingly, but I shook my head.

"How about you, Anne?" he asked. "Want a ride?"

Anne took my cue and shook her head but added, "I can swim beside you." She didn't want to be left out completely.

"OK," agreed Matt. "Here we go." He started out in a slow crawl, slow enough that Anne had no trouble keeping up with him.

"He's neat, Jenny," said Tina. "Do you think he'd take me across again?"

"He might," I replied. "If you ask him nicely, that is."

For the next half hour I sat on the edge of the pool, just watching as Matt played with the girls. And while I didn't look at Brad more than a couple of times, I was acutely aware that he was watching us. I wished we had asked him to join us.

When Matt finally pulled himself up to sit beside me, he said, "They're wild. Especially Tina. But I like them."

"They like you, too," I told him. "And why wouldn't they? They haven't had this much attention all summer."

"They're good kids, but I'd rather pay more attention to you." Matt smiled down at me with that same twinkle in his eyes. "How about tonight, Jenny? Are you busy?"

"No."

"Then how about going somewhere? Taking in a movie or something?"

I thought about his not having a job and said, "How about the 'something'? Suppose I show you around?"

"It's a date. What time? Is seven too early?"

"Seven is fine," I said.

As Matt and Brad left, Anne turned to me and said, "I think I'm in love, Jenny."

I just smiled fondly at her. But I thought I might be, too. There was something natural and unassuming about Matt, something so likable and endearing that it would be hard not to love him—given half a chance.

Did Brad have the same qualities? I wondered. Beneath his reserve, was Brad just as exciting as Matt was? It was an intriguing question.

What had started out as a routine, rather boring summer was suddenly turning into a very exciting one.

Chapter Four

I decided to wear jeans that night instead of shorts. It had been pretty hot during the day, but I knew that in the late evening the breeze could get cool.

When Matt arrived, I took him into the den and introduced him to my parents. They always liked to know who I went out with.

I'd gotten so I could pretty much tell what my parents thought of my dates just by their expressions. I could tell right away that Mom approved of Matt. She doesn't like long hair or sloppy clothes, and Matt wasn't guilty of either of those faults.

I'd have to wait until the next day to get Dad's opinion, but he didn't look displeased. He prefers boys who look him in the eye and have a firm handshake. I couldn't tell about the handshake, but Matt had certainly been straightforward enough.

Nevertheless, Dad still had to say, "Don't forget you have to go to work in the morning, Jenny."

I couldn't help smiling as I said, "I won't." I suppose that if I had a daughter, I'd be protective, too.

"Where to?" asked Matt when we got into the car.

I'd been thinking about that ever since Matt asked me out. There isn't a whole lot to do in our southern Indiana valley, at least not for valley folk, which is what I was—and what Matt was now, too. Ours is a resort town, which means there are two kinds of people, tourists and natives. A lot of the natives work at the resort, but when they get off work, they don't hang around the hotel or the grounds.

I thought Matt would be more interested in local people than in tourist traffic, so I suggested we go to Charlie's Cookout, which is where most of my friends go. It was once a barn, but Charlie converted it into a restaurant. It has outdoor charcoal fires, where he cooks the best hot dogs and hamburgers in town. Inside, Charlie left hay bales in the rafters and straw on the floor to give the place some atmosphere. The restaurant draws its share of tourists, but most of them cluster around Charlie, listening to his tales. We locals have heard all of them, so we gather in the barn, in booths close to the Coke bar. The first person I saw when we got inside was Melissa Barkley. She's a tall, striking-looking blond, and she's easy to spot. Sitting next to her was Guy Farrow, the boy she goes with.

Until Melissa began dating regularly, back in the eighth grade, she was one of the "Regent Street Regulars." That's what Elaine Foster, Jody Moore, Melissa, and I used to call ourselves. We were inseparable all through grade school. Where one went, the other three followed.

We were still close, but we didn't get together as often as we used to, especially in the summer. Between jobs, dating, and vacations, it was really hard to find the time. Elaine was out of town for the month of August, Jody worked in a shop at the mall until nine at night, and after Melissa found Guy, she drifted away from the rest of us.

Melissa spotted us immediately and waved a hand in a come-here gesture.

"You might as well meet some of the gang," I told Matt, giving him a resigned smile. It was always nice to run into Melissa and Guy, but right then I would rather have been alone with Matt. After all, it was our first real date.

"Why not?" said Matt, grinning.

I led the way to Melissa and Guy's booth and noticed a few of the other kids watching with interest as we made our way between tables. It made me proud to be with Matt.

When I introduced him to Melissa and Guy, Melissa widened her eyes and gave Matt a long, slow smile. The boys shook hands, but I could sense a wariness on Guy's part. If Matt noticed it, he didn't let on.

"So what have you been doing since you got here?" asked Melissa, resting her chin on her hands and gazing charmingly at Matt. That kind of flirting was automatic and unconscious with her. Elaine, Jody, and I used to tease her about it but that didn't do any good. She couldn't help being innocently flirtatious. And it didn't bother anyone, except Guy, of course.

He was watching Matt with slightly narrowed eyes. He was crazy about Melissa, and he hated the thought of her flirting with another guy, even innocently.

Matt smiled disarmingly and answered Melissa's question. "Getting acquainted." Then he looked down at me, his eyes sparkling.

"You'll be a senior?" Guy must have relaxed because he sounded genuinely interested in Matt.

"Yes," said Matt.

"Going out for any sports?" asked Guy.

When Matt told him football, Guy relaxed even more. According to Melissa, Guy was sure to be MVP in basketball that year. There wasn't a better athlete on the team. Of course, someone new could always move to town, and Matt was not only built well, he was also a couple of inches taller than Guy.

If Melissa noticed Matt's lack of interest in her, she wasn't offended. "Why haven't I seen you around before?" she asked.

"Brad and I have been pretty busy."

"Brad?"

"My twin brother," explained Matt.

"Are you identical twins?" asked Melissa.

"Not identical. We just look alike."

"And where is Brad?" she asked, glancing around the room and sitting up a little straighter.

"Brad had something else to do," answered Matt.

We sat down with them, had Cokes, and talked for about half an hour and then excused ourselves. "Jenny's showing me the town," said Matt as he waited for me to get out of the booth.

When we climbed into the car, Matt turned to me and grinned. "Does Melissa mean it when she flirts so outrageously?"

"No," I said and laughed. "Not at all. She's just as crazy about Guy as he is about her. She wouldn't think of going out with anyone else. It's just her way. You have to get to know her."

"I think I'll pass on that. How about just cruising for a while?"

That was fine with me. We drove around aimlessly until finally Matt turned into the circular driveway that swept up to the front of the resort's hotel.

"Scoot down," he ordered as we approached the long canopy where a tall, red-uniformed doorman waited.

"Why?" I asked, obeying his instructions and slipping lower in the seat.

"You don't want anyone to recognize you in this old car, do you? It might spoil your image."

I laughed and straightened back up. "For a minute there I thought you were serious." I would have been happy to be seen with Matt anywhere, in anything, by anyone.

Matt didn't stop until we left the circular drive, and then he just pulled over to the curb and left the motor running as he looked back at the front of the hotel.

"It's too modern, doesn't fit in here. Too much glass and too many lights. It looks out of place in a sleepy valley town."

"Sleepy?" I asked.

"Yes. You know. Quiet, peaceful."

"You, sir," I said with mock indignation, "are speaking of the former Las Vegas of the Midwest."

Matt raised one eyebrow and gave me a skeptical look.

"You don't believe me, do you? OK, I'll show you. Just make a left at the next corner and follow the road." I hadn't intended to take him to the old Valley Spa as it's a favorite make-out spot, and I didn't want him to think I was fast. Yet I didn't want him to think I was making anything up, either.

We drove for about three miles. Then I told him to slow down and turn through a stone arch. On the other side was a wide, brick-paved boulevard.

"What's this?" he asked.

"It's just a tourist attraction now. They give guided tours of it in the summer," I explained. "But it used to be a famous spa and gambling casino. There, up ahead on the right, is the main building."

As we approached it, we could easily make out the huge white columns at the front entrance, but the rest of the building blended in with the night.

There were a few scattered streetlights, but the only effect they had was to deepen the shadows. "It's too dark to see much now," I said. "We'll have to come back in the daylight."

As we followed the boulevard around a flagpole, Matt's headlights swept across a car parked on one of the side roads. There was a couple in it.

"Are those tourists?" asked Matt innocently. His tone told me that he knew otherwise, that he was only kidding.

"I doubt it," I said, laughing softly. "They're probably locals. Sometimes I think this place is even more popular at night than it is in the daytime." I knew that we could have found more parked cars if we'd wanted to.

Matt slowed the car to a crawl as we went back past the old hotel. He was peering through his side window at the ghostly looking building. Then he stopped the car completely.

"It's on the national registry of historic places," I added. But I wasn't really thinking about the old hotel. I was thinking about Matt and me and where we were. I was wondering what he was thinking and if he'd kiss me.

So I was a little startled when he said softly, "Brad would love it."

"What?" I asked, thinking I must have misunderstood.

"Brad would love it." Matt turned to face me, and even in the dim light I could see the enthusiasm in his eyes. "He's a real history nut. Would you show him around, Jenny?"

"Well, sure," I said, a little taken aback. "If you think he'd like it." I was disappointed that Matt seemed more interested in his twin than in me.

There we were, just the two of us, in a romantic setting at a romantic time of night, and Matt's mind was on his brother! It really jarred me. I was thinking about Matt so hard that it didn't occur to me that his thoughts might be elsewhere. And yet I knew he was interested in me. If he weren't he wouldn't have come to my house, wouldn't have asked me to go to the pool with him, and wouldn't have taken me out, would he?

"How about tomorrow?" I offered. "It's Saturday, so we could go anytime."

"Great. What time should we pick you up?"

"We?" I repeated.

"Of course. Brad and me. I'm interested, too, you know."

His smile was so disarming that I had to fight down an impulse to reach up and touch him.

Chapter Five

I was sitting on the curb, tying another knot in my shoelaces when Matt and Brad drove up. Matt and I had talked earlier and decided that he and Brad would pick me up around ten.

Matt got out of the car and held the door open while I climbed in to sit between him and Brad, who was driving.

"This is really nice of you, Jenny," said Brad with a sideward glance as we set off down the street. "Matt told me about the old resort, and I'm really anxious to see it."

"I think you'll like it," I told him.

We were a little cramped in the small car until Matt put his arm along the back of the front seat. Out of the corner of my eye, I glanced from Matt to Brad and back. Again I felt a little giddy sitting between two such good-looking guys. The fact that they looked so alike was even more disturbing. It made me wish I were a twin, too, so I could date both of them.

"Slow down a little," I said to Brad when we got to the edge of town. "We're almost there. The entrance is a little hard to spot unless you know just where to look. There. Make the next right."

Brad turned, and then he stepped on the brake, stopping to study the yellow brick arch. In the stone at the top of the arch was carved Valley Spa Hotel. The red brick boulevard stretched under the arch and disappeared over a small rise.

"Very impressive," Brad remarked.

"I'm afraid it's not what it used to be, but we think it's pretty nice." There was pride in my voice, and I suddenly wished I knew more about the old hotel.

"This hotel didn't have nearly so many rooms as the new one at the resort, but it was a lot more exclusive," I said when we reached the front of the hotel. Brad parked the car, and we all got out and gazed up at the magnificent columned structure. Since it was still pretty early in the morning, we had the place to ourselves, except for the guards.

"It sort of dwarfs us, doesn't it?" stated Brad, his voice filled with awe.

"Yes," I said. "It got pretty run-down until it was designated a historical monument, and then we were able to get funds to restore it. But there's still a lot of work to be done."

"Look at that," said Matt, pointing to a wide, white veranda that clung to the sides of the building and disappeared around a curve.

"The shape of the veranda was determined by the dome," I explained. "You can't see it from here, but it's really huge. At the time the hotel was built, it was the largest unsupported dome in the world. Why don't we go inside and take a look at it?" I suggested.

"This I have to see," said Brad, racing up the steps ahead of Matt and me.

"I told you he'd like it," Matt said, looking down at me and smiling as we followed Brad into the building past the guard.

When we reached Brad, he was standing spellbound, gazing at the enormous dome that covered a circular room large enough to house a circus.

I couldn't tell whether the glow on his face came from the light through the glass of the dome or from himself. Whichever it was, it gave me a funny sensation to watch him. He looked so appealing. Mentally shaking myself,

I brushed off the feeling. Then I smiled at Matt, and we followed Brad around the room, pausing when he did to study statues, alcoves, marble facings, and intricate patterns in the tile floor. His enthusiasm was contagious.

"Let's go out the side door," I said. "And we can walk back on the porch."

To the left of the hotel was an area about the size of a city block. The center was a large garden filled with multicolored flowers and crisscrossed with red brick paths. On either side of the garden was a round building encased by tall white pillars. At the end and stretching the full width of the garden was the bowling pavilion. All three buildings were of yellow brick with green tile roofs.

We took one of the side paths through the garden until we came to the first building. I had been watching both boys, waiting for a reaction, and when I saw Matt wrinkle his nose, I laughed.

"It's the springs," I told him. "Come on." I ran ahead of them into the gazebo-style building. In the very center of it was a pool of water that bubbled up and spilled over into a trough. The pool was surrounded by a circular seat of ceramic tile.

"Whew!" exclaimed Matt. "What kind of spring is that? It smells like rotten eggs."

"A sulfur spring," I said. "That's what this whole place was all about. The gambling was just a side attraction. What really brought people here was the springs. Most of them have been capped, but this one was left open for tourists."

"People paid to see something like this?" asked Matt. He leaned over the pool and then drew back and shuddered. "What did they do with it?"

"Some people bathed in it. It was thought to be very beneficial. Supposedly it'd cure anything and everything."

"I'd have to have a good long shower after that," said Matt, joking.

"And some people drank it," I added with a wicked grin.

"You're putting me on," said Matt, scowling.

"No, I'm not. If I had a glass—"

"Here are some cups," said Brad. He had found a cup dispenser while Matt and I had been talking, and he pulled out three paper cups. I had never noticed the dispenser before. It must have been added during the restoration. I was almost sorry I had mentioned it, but it was too late to back down.

Brad knelt down by the side of the pool

and scooped up a small cupful of water. Then he raised it to his lips and took a drink.

"What does it taste like?" asked Matt.

"Pretty good, really. Try it," said Brad.

Matt scooped up a little of the sulfur water, and I did the same. I took a sip and tried not to smell the vapors. Even so, the first swallow was something I'd rather forget. The second wasn't quite so awful, but by the time I got to the third, I was back to my original opinion.

"Whose idea was this?" asked Matt, making a face and tossing his empty cup into a plastic trash container.

Brad and I both said, "Not mine!" at the same time, and then we all three burst out laughing.

Brad's quick denial both surprised and delighted me. It was more like something Matt would have said. When I glanced in his direction, I saw that he was staring at Matt, a teasing expression in his eyes. Matt gave him a grin and held up one finger as if to say, "That's one for you."

For just a second I felt a little left out, but then I reminded myself that they were very close. They had shared many special moments.

Brad sobered up quicker than Matt did, but his surprising response gave me an insight into his character. Maybe he wasn't really as solemn as he appeared to be. Maybe it was just a case of getting to know him better.

I was still thinking about Brad and how complex he was when we came to the bowling pavilion. It was locked so we couldn't do anything except peer into the dark interior through the windows. The room was very long and narrow, and I tried to imagine how it would look with bowling alleys and tenpins.

"Jenny!" Matt whispered urgently.

He had a finger to his lips as I turned around. Then he pointed to the ground. A small green salamander was sitting on one of the stones near the walk.

"He's yours if I can catch him," said Matt, reaching down very slowly and not taking his eyes off the small animal. His hand was still more than a foot from the tiny lizard when it darted away. Matt went after it, and I followed, but every time we got within reaching distance, the salamander darted ahead. Finally it disappeared behind a bush.

"Sorry about that," said Matt. "I really thought I could catch it."

I shrugged. "Oh, well. Maybe it's just as well. I took a frog home once, and poor Baffin nearly lost his mind trying to catch it to see what it was. I wonder how he'd react to a salamander."

"It would probably frighten him half to death," said Matt with a big grin.

"You're getting to know him all right."

We were both laughing when we came around the corner of the building in search of Brad. We had left him peering through one of the windows of the pavilion, and that's where we found him. He hadn't moved.

"What's the score, Brad?" asked Matt.

"I wasn't counting." Brad moved away from the window, smiling a little sheepishly at me. "I was just watching."

I must have looked a little confused, for Matt draped one arm over my shoulder and said, "Brad is very intense sometimes. If he were anyone else, I'd say he sees things that aren't there."

"But they are there, you know," Brad stated solemnly. "It just takes a little imagination and some concentration."

"Imagination I have," said Matt. "But as for concentration, give me something real to concentrate on. Or should I say 'someone' real?" He winked at me and gave me a secretive smile.

"Well," I said, trying to retain my composure, "that's about it unless you want to hike up to the observatory. It's on the other side of the hotel and up a pretty steep hill."

"I'd like to see it," said Brad.

"I think I'll sit right here on this nice brick wall and wait," said Matt. He patted the spot beside him and raised his eyebrows at me.

"Me, too," I said. "Just follow the dirt path, Brad. You can't miss it."

Brad struck off up the path, and I sat down by Matt. I had enjoyed the outing with both of the boys. And Matt was right, they really were different. What I had thought was mere shyness in Brad was not that at all.

It was a lot more complicated than that. I had seen the way he had gazed at the dome—rapt, enthralled, fascinated. And at the spring he was curious, curious enough to taste the water on his own and smart enough to trick Matt and me into tasting it.

I smiled to myself as I remembered. Matt had taken the joke good-naturedly. I would have been surprised and disappointed if he hadn't. I hadn't known him very long, but his actions and his words so far had shown me that he was a very considerate and thoughtful person.

The word *thoughtful* made me think of Brad again, especially the way he had looked when he turned away from the pavilion window. There was something in his eyes—something he had seen that we hadn't.

I liked them both. Each one was appealing in his own very special way. I wished I were twins, too!

Matt and I talked for a while, and then we both fell silent, easy and comfortable with each other. Finally I noticed that we had been sitting there for quite a while.

"What's keeping Brad?" I asked. "You don't suppose he got lost, do you? Or that he might have fallen and be in trouble?" I was beginning to worry about him.

"He's all right," Matt assured me. "You don't know him. He's probably charting the heavens in that observatory. When he gets wrapped up in something, he forgets time."

"I see what you mean about you and Brad just looking alike. Inside, you're not at all alike, are you?"

"Oh, basically we are. We have the same values and all, but I'm a here-and-now person. I relate more to people than to places and things. Brad—"

"Here he comes." I hadn't meant to interrupt, but I was so relieved to see him that I couldn't help it.

"It's about time," said Matt, getting up

and pulling me to my feet. "Jenny was getting worried about you."

Brad apologized but offered no reason for his long absence other than the fact that he had forgotten what time it was. There was that same air of suppressed excitement about him that fascinated me.

Matt drove home with me in the middle again. Brad was extremely quiet. Most of the time he stared out through the side window, but I had a feeling he wasn't really seeing anything we passed. I thought he was still back at Valley Spa, not just a few minutes earlier, but maybe a hundred years or so earlier. I wondered if I'd ever find out.

Chapter Six

Matt didn't come over that night nor the next day, but he did call. Part of our conversation was about his brother.

"You made quite an impression on Brad, Jenny."

"Me?" I asked dumbly. "Or the old hotel?"

"That, too, but he actually told our parents about you, and he almost never mentions a girl's name. That's how I knew he was impressed."

I hadn't set out to impress Brad, and I had no idea what I'd done to make him think well of me, but whatever it was, I was glad it had happened.

"Well, he made an impression on me, too," I said honestly. "I really liked him."

After we hung up, I wrote a long letter to

my friend, Elaine, who was visiting some relatives in California. In it I told her all about the boys and the time we had spent together.

The only thing I left out in my letter to Elaine was that I was having a hard time deciding which boy I liked more. But I'm sure she could read between the lines. We'd been friends for a long time.

The following Monday morning I shivered and snuggled back under the covers after shutting off the alarm. The temperature had dropped during the night, and the breeze coming through my open window was almost cold. I hated to get out of my warm bed.

"Jenny!" called Mom. "Are you up?"

"Yes," I said, throwing back the covers and rushing to the window to close it. *Too cold to swim today*, I thought.

I stayed in the hot shower until I felt warm. Then I put on a pair of jeans and a blue checkered shirt with long sleeves that I rolled up.

When I got to the Carltons' and Tina saw how I was dressed, she was really disappointed.

"Where's your swimsuit?" she demanded.

"At home," I said. "It's too cold to go

swimming." I shivered and wrapped my arms around myself to emphasize the point.

"No, it's not," insisted Tina.

"You haven't been outside," I told her. "It's only sixty-five."

"Sixty-five is warm. Couldn't you go home and get it?" she asked beseechingly.

"Jenny's right," said Anne. "It's too cold. Besides, the pool doesn't even open if it gets below seventy." She tried to reason with Tina, but I knew that she was disappointed, too.

"There's always tomorrow," I said brightly, ruffling Tina's hair.

"Yeah. But what about today?"

"Well," I said, "we could always play cards or go for a walk or—go to the movies! How about seeing that new movie at the mall? I hear it's pretty good."

Anne shrugged her shoulders. "OK with me." Then she turned to her sister and said, "What do you think, Tina. Do you want to go?"

Tina nodded and smiled, her mood lightening. "All right."

"Great!" I cried. "And we have plenty of time to stop by the library first."

"The library!" shrieked Tina. "What for?"

"Books, dummy, what else?" asked Anne, with more resignation than indignation.

Just the same, I gave her a stern look for

calling her sister a dummy, and she apologized.

"I'm sorry," Anne mumbled. "I didn't really mean you're dumb. I just thought it was kind of obvious, that's all."

Tina accepted the apology silently, and then Anne went on, "I'm not too thrilled about going to the library, either, Jenny, but if you really want to go I guess we'll have to tag along. I suppose you want to get another romance novel. Maybe I should start reading them," she added thoughtfully.

A lot of girls her age did, but I neither encouraged nor discouraged her. Reading is too personal. There is reading, and then there is *reading*. The first is the kind you do for information, like in school. The second is the kind you do for enjoyment. It's a form of escaping into another world. Maybe the world I liked to escape to wasn't the world someone else would want.

I had finished *Always in Love* and was satisfied with the ending even though it didn't come about quite the way I thought it would. . . .

Marcie had been surprised and upset when report cards came out and she had C's in everything except chemistry. I could understand her being upset, but she shouldn't have been surprised. And she knew she really didn't deserve the A she got in chem. There were too many times when she hadn't been prepared for the experiments and Cary had bailed her out. Oh, he didn't cheat for her or anything like that, but he certainly did more than his share of the work.

In the end Marcie had done a lot of soul searching and finally realized that she'd been kidding herself. She'd been pretending to like Allen's fast, easygoing style, but the only times she'd really felt relaxed and content were the times she was with Cary.

Breaking off with Allen had been easy. Marcie had thought the hard part would be telling Cary how much she really liked him, but actually it wasn't hard at all. He had known all along that he and Marcie were meant for each other. He had only been waiting for her to realize it. I would have liked Cary to have been a little more aggressive, but it just wasn't in his nature.

Since we had the time, I went home on the way to the library to pick up the book. I figured I might as well return it before it became overdue. I ran inside while the girls waited in the car. Then we were on our way.

When we got to the library, we split up. Tina and Anne went to the children's room while I headed for the young adult section. For a small-town library, it was remarkably well stocked, and I always had plenty of titles to choose from.

I hadn't noticed anyone else around, so I jumped when I heard someone say, "Jenny!" in a loud whisper.

The voice was familiar and when I wheeled around and saw who it was, I grinned. "Matt!"

"Brad," he said, his smile faltering a little.

I felt myself getting pink with embarrassment. "Of course, Brad. I guess I spoke before I looked."

"It's OK," he said, recovering quickly and giving me the shy smile that I was beginning to find enchanting. "I'm used to it."

"I didn't expect to see you here," I told him.

"Actually, I spend quite a bit of time in libraries. I'm not very familiar with this one yet, though."

That wasn't exactly what I meant. I just hadn't expected to see him in that section, the romance section. Then I saw him glance at the shelves behind me, the reference shelves, and I felt foolish. It wasn't romance novels he was interested in; it was the encyclopedias! I should have known that right away from his interest in history.

"Are you looking for anything in particular?" I asked.

Brad looked a little sheepish. Then he said, "I thought I might find something more on the spa. Not that you didn't do a good job of showing us around," he added gallantly.

"Maybe I can help you," I offered. "Have you been through the Indiana section yet?"

"No," he said, his eyes lighting up. "I didn't know there was one."

"It's in a corner at the back of the stacks. Come on. I'll show you."

Brad followed me past the fiction section to a tall bookcase labeled Indiana History. Most of the books were old, with dark covers and faded inscriptions.

"They're arranged by author," I explained. "I did a report once on the spa, but it was a long time ago—in the seventh grade, I think. I wish I could remember the author of the book I used, but I don't. In fact, I don't even remember the title."

"I've already looked in the card catalog," said Brad. "But I didn't find anything about the hotel listed there."

"No, you wouldn't. I don't think anyone has written a whole book just on the spa.

Darn! If only I could remember where I found all that information."

"I guess we'll just have to look through the indexes."

When Brad said "we," I glanced up at him. There was a small window behind him, and it threw his face in shadow so I couldn't see his expression too well, but I could tell that he wasn't looking at me. I don't think he was even conscious that he had included me in his search.

"I'll start on this side, and you start on that," I said, glad to be of help.

We began opening one book after another in search of any reference to the spa or to our area. The ones I knew wouldn't help, I skipped, such as *Birds of Indiana* and *The Indiana Constitution*.

"Look for the name Lystrom, too," I suggested. "That's the man who built the spa, and a lot of other things around here."

"Uh-huh," mumbled Brad, engrossed in his search.

When I came to a book titled *An Atlas of Southern Indiana* with the subtitle, *A Guide to Small Towns and Villages, 1850–1900*, a bell rang in my head. I took the book down, found Spring Waters in the index, and turned to the numbered page.

I was about to say "this is it" when I came to a picture that almost took my breath away. There was the tall young man in a frock coat and top hat lending an arm to a lady about to step down from a carriage.

It was a very clear picture, considering how old it must have been. The young man was looking at the lady, his face in profile. It was a strong face, almost rugged. I turned toward Brad, intending to show him the picture, and gasped. He had turned sideways so that the small window made a perfect frame for his profile. He could have posed for the picture in the book.

"Did you find something?" he asked, turning to face me.

I had a hard time controlling my voice. "I—I'm not sure," I said. "But I think so."

"What is it?"

I showed him the title of the book, keeping my finger between the pages, and then I showed him the picture.

"It's certainly the right period," he said. "Look how they're dressed. Is that the spa in the background?"

I hadn't paid any attention to the background, so I leaned a little closer to him as we both peered at the page. "It could be," I said.

"But it's hard to tell. And there isn't any legend for the picture."

"What's going on?" asked a small voice behind us. Brad and I both jumped.

"Tina!" I exclaimed. "You startled us. You shouldn't sneak up on people."

"I wasn't sneaking up. You just weren't paying any attention. Can we go now?"

"Yes, sure," I said. I handed to book to Brad. "I'm pretty sure this is the one I used, but you might find something else if you want to look some more."

"I think I will, but I want this one, too. Thanks for your help, Jenny." Brad turned back to the bookshelf, as Tina and I headed for the checkout table, where Anne, who was almost as impatient as Tina, was waiting. I collected Anne and quickly ushered the girls out the door.

During the movie, I couldn't get the picture in the book out of my mind. The resemblance between the two boys' profiles was uncanny. It made shivers run down my spine. I could see the picture just as clearly as if it were still in front of me—the young man, who might have been an earlier version of Brad, and the young lady, who, with a little imagination, could have been me.

Chapter Seven

That night I was finishing the dinner dishes when the phone rang. It was Matt.

"Do you have any plans for tonight?" he asked.

"Nothing definite. I thought I might walk over to the ball park."

"Mind if I tag along with you?"

"Of course I don't mind," I said.

He sounded so cheerful that I couldn't wait to be with him. I had been brooding too much about my reaction to that picture in the library, and I was ready for some simple, uncomplicated fun. I knew that Matt was the perfect person to shake me out of my peculiar mood.

We must have walked two or three miles that night, but it didn't seem like it. We stopped at the ball park, and I introduced Matt to some more of the gang, who were gathered around the concession stand between games.

"You play any softball?" asked Brent Chambers after he and Matt shook hands. "We can always use some extra players, and you look as if you could really hit the ball a long way." Brent was manager of the summer league, and he was always on the lookout for new prospects.

"I used to play Little League some, but that's hardball," said Matt.

Brent's round, freckled face broke into a grin. "There's not all that much difference. Come around some afternoon. We practice from three to five."

"I'll try to make it," promised Matt.

George Stillwell, who was a substitute guard at the pool, spoke up. "I'd be glad to pick you up any afternoon if you don't have a way here. Where do you live?"

I felt a tug on my arm, and when I turned away from Matt and the boys I found myself face to face with two girls from school.

"Where did you find him?" asked Julie Stern, her gray eyes wide with delight.

"And, more to the point, are there any more at home like him?" asked Sally Farlow, her pretty face aglow as she peered over my shoulder to get a better look at Matt.

"As a matter of fact, there are," I told them, giggling. "Or there is. He has a twin brother, Brad."

"Lead me to him," said Julie with a deep sigh.

"Me, too," echoed Sally.

I laughed at their eagerness, knowing that if I had been them and they had been me, I would have felt the same way. As it was, I was enjoying being the center of attention. I was also enjoying the fact that they seemed to consider that because Matt and I arrived together, we were going together. It made me feel warm inside.

At the start of the second game, the gang broke up and began to drift back to the grandstand.

"Want to sit with us?" offered Brent.

"Thanks, but I don't think we'll stay," answered Matt. "Unless you want to?" He looked at me, and I shook my head almost imperceptibly. "It was nice meeting you," Matt said as he shook Brent's hand again. "Maybe another time."

"Don't forget about practice, three to five, weekdays," called Brent as we started away.

"If I can't make practice, I'll at least stop by to say hello," Matt promised.

From the way Matt fit in, you would have thought he had known my friends as long as I had. I wondered if he had ever been a stranger.

When we finally wound up back at my house, I asked Matt if he wanted to come in, but he said he had better get on home. Then he took my chin in his hand and lifted my face up toward his.

"Jenny, Jenny," he said, smiling down at me. "You just might be the loveliest girl I've ever met."

"Might?" I asked, feigning displeasure at his even doubting it.

"Might!" he repeated, grinning. Then he kissed me lightly on the forehead and said good night. I stood on the porch for another five minutes or so before I sighed happily and went inside. I hadn't thought about "the picture" again all evening.

"Do my eyes deceive me?" asked Mom when I walked into the kitchen the next day right after Dad had left for work. "Is that my daughter, Jenny, standing there?" Mom opened her eyes wide in disbelief. She wasn't used to seeing me up before nine-thirty.

"It's me, all right," I said, opening the

refrigerator for some milk. "I want to go to the library before I go over to the Carltons'." I had been so rattled the day before after finding that book for Brad that I had forgotten to get one for me.

And even if I had remembered, I wouldn't have had time. Tina and Anne were anxious to leave, and I didn't like to pick just any book off the shelf. I tried to get some idea of what the hero was like by reading the little blurbs on the cover.

I had my own notion of the ideal boy. His physical features often changed. Sometimes he was tall, and sometimes he was not so tall. His eyes could have been blue or brown or gray, maybe even green or hazel. And he might have been a blond or a brunette, although right then I was leaning toward a tall blond boy with blue eyes.

"I'm fresh out of books," I told Mom. I sat down beside her and reached for my morning doughnut.

"One of these days you're going to turn into a book," she said teasingly. "You must take after your father. He loves to read, too. I never seem to find the time."

My mother is a small, attractive, vivacious woman. She has enough energy for two people. She keeps our big, old house in tip-top shape, fixes fantastic meals, serves on several committees and charities, volunteers at the Retirement Center, and still has time for Dad and me.

I enjoy my father, too, but in a different way. He's quiet and reserved where Mom is outgoing. He doesn't mind spending a peaceful evening at home, though my mother can't stand to have time on her hands. Sometimes I wonder how they ever got together.

"I'll go straight from the library to the Carltons', Mom," I said as I got up to put my glass in the sink.

I was almost late to pick up Anne and Tina. I must have looked at a couple dozen books before I finally selected the two I wanted.

Anne and Tina were waiting for me on the front steps, so we got to the pool in record time. I spotted Brad right away. I knew it was him because of the precise way he was springing from the diving board, smoothly slicing into the water. He really was quite good. After I had spread my towel on the deck, I looked over again and saw Brad climbing the ladder for another dive. When he turned his head my way, I waved. He smiled and waved back.

About fifteen minutes later, he left the

deep end, swimming underwater until he surfaced right in front of me.

"Hi," he said warmly. His wet hair was slicked back, and he was slightly out of breath.

"Hi." I tried to think of something witty to say but for one of the few times in my life, I was tongue-tied.

"Matt's out looking for a job."

"You don't have to explain," I said, feeling foolish for even saying it. It sounded too much like I was telling him, in an oblique way, that I didn't care, that I was just as interested in him as I was in Matt. *Well, are you?* a little voice inside asked. I shook my head from side to side and uttered a silent *no*.

"Is something wrong?" asked Brad, looking confused and concerned.

"No, no, of course not." I gave him a bright smile. "The picture" had flashed across my mind again, and I had felt a chill in spite of the warm summer sun beating down on my back. A chill, or shivers of excitement?

"Did you find the information you were looking for yesterday?" I asked.

"Yes," he replied, "thanks to you." He smiled at me so appreciatively that I felt more confused than ever. I turned the conversation back to Matt.

"What kind of job is Matt looking for?" I was hoping he didn't notice how flustered I was.

"Any kind. But what he really wants is to work at the hotel."

"How about you?" I asked. "Have you applied there, too, or do you have something else already sewn up?"

"Nothing definite," said Brad. He tried to sound nonchalant, but there was a note of excitement in his voice. "I've got a pretty good chance of getting one at the *Times-Mail*. I had an interview this morning."

"That's great, Brad!" I exclaimed. "What kind of work would you be doing? News stories?"

"No. Nothing like that. Have you read any of the 'Then and Now' columns?"

"Sometimes. Not very often, though." The column was about the history of our area.

Brad was still standing in the waist-deep water while I sat on the edge of the deck. I wished he would get out and sit down beside me where we could talk a little more privately. Not that I had anything private to say. I just felt a little awkward with me sitting and him standing.

"I told the editor about some of the ideas I had for making comparisons between life in the nineteenth century and life in the twentieth. I told him I'd do all the research myself in my spare time."

Out of the corner of my eye, I saw Tina and Anne making their way toward us. "That sounds interesting, Brad," I said a bit loudly, emphasizing his name. I didn't want the girls to rush up and call him Matt as I had at the library. It must be unnerving to constantly be taken for your twin, even if you are used to it.

"Carry me through the deep end?" Tina asked Brad when she reached him. She flashed him a fetching smile.

"Sure," said Brad. He squatted down so that Tina could get her hands on his shoulders, and then he swam very carefully and cautiously across the pool and back.

Anne waited patiently for her turn.

As I watched them, I thought about the way Matt had taken to the girls. It was obvious Brad liked them, too, but he didn't have the easy camaraderie with them that Matt had. Matt's actions were spontaneous. It had been he who had initiated the water play and the girls who had followed his lead. With Brad it was the other way around. He followed their suggestions and, while he seemed to be enjoying himself, I got the impression that he was holding something back.

"He's nice," said Anne as Brad towed Tina across the pool for the last time. "But I like the other one better."

"Why?" I asked, wishing I could make such a positive statement myself.

"I don't know exactly. But Matt's more—more—more . . ." She finally gave up searching for the word and just shrugged her shoulders. "You know what I mean."

I couldn't think of the word either, so I mumbled, "Uh-huh," which didn't mean that I agreed, only that I knew they were different.

I thought about the book I had just finished, *Always in Love*, and how much I had admired the hero, Cary. Could Matt have played the part of Cary? I wondered. I tried to imagine him as that hero, but there was something that didn't fit. No, Matt was too outgoing, too much like Allen, only without Allen's shallowness. In fact, if Allen had had some of Matt's qualities, he might have been almost perfect.

Now Brad. Yes, Brad could have played the part of Cary. In fact, Brad could have been Cary. They were both reserved, quiet, and thoughtful, with a deep sense of integrity. It was quite appealing, I realized. And considering my feelings for Matt, quite confusing, too.

Chapter Eight

I didn't see or hear from either of the twins on Wednesday or Thursday so I had plenty of time to read the two books I had picked up at the library.

In the first one, the hero was a rather studious boy named Larry. At the beginning I thought he was going to be dull. But then his more appealing qualities began to show through. He reminded me of Brad.

The hero in the second book, Billy, was more outgoing. At least that was how he was described at first. He was active and popular, involved in sports and school activities. But I later found out he had to work at covering up his shyness.

He and the heroine, Tammy, had known each other for a long time and had dated casually. They both dated other people, too. Tammy thought Billy was a lot of fun, but she didn't take him seriously until she was in an accident and it was Billy, fun-loving, irresponsible Billy, who stood by her. If it hadn't been for the accident she might never have known the real Billy—a boy with deep, tender feelings, the kind of boy she had been looking for all along.

When I closed the second book, I thought how Billy's shy side reminded me of Brad. I sat up a little straighter in my armchair. What was I thinking? Both of the heroes in those books made me think of Brad. Was it prophetic? Would I eventually wind up with Brad? Maybe he was waiting for me to realize how I felt. Then I shook my head and told myself I'd been reading too many books.

I got up from the chair, stretched, and was thinking about calling Melissa or Jody when the phone rang. It was Matt.

"What are you doing, Jenny?" he asked.

"I was reading, but I just finished my book," I told him. He didn't mention the past days or what he'd been doing during that time, and I didn't ask.

"How about a movie at the drive-in?"

"Great!" I said. All thoughts of Brad vanished from my head.

"I'll see you at seven-thirty."

Matt arrived right on time, looking better than ever. He had on a pale yellow polo shirt and black jeans.

"What's the movie?" I asked as he helped me into the car.

"I don't know," Matt replied. He got in, started the ignition, and pulled away from the curb. "I guess we'll find out when we get there." There was a secretive smile on his face, and then suddenly it vanished. "I'm sorry, Jenny. I should have checked first. Maybe it's something you've already seen."

"If it is, we can always do something else," I said agreeably.

"No." Matt pounded his fist on the steering wheel in frustration. "I promised you a movie. We'd be too late for any other show. I was so anxious to see you that I didn't even think about what was playing."

"Well, why don't we drive out there and see what it is?" I suggested.

"Good idea." The smile was back on his face.

I wondered why he was so anxious to see me. I waited for him to say something, but he drove along in silence. He seemed excited. Finally I couldn't stand it any longer.

"What are you so wound up about? Has something happened?" I asked.

"Yes." Matt took his eyes from the road long enough to grin at me, and I got caught up in his enthusiasm. His eyes sparkled, and he squeezed the steering wheel harder as we turned into the theater.

"Well?"

"Wait till we find a spot. I want to see your expression, and I can't watch you and the road at the same time."

Matt paid for the tickets, drove on in, and found a spot near the screen. After he had switched off the ignition, he turned sideways, took my hand, and squeezed it. "I got the job!" he said exuberantly. "The one I really wanted!"

"At the hotel?" I asked, remembering what Brad had said about Matt's wanting to work there.

"How did you know?" he asked tonelessly.

He sounded so disappointed that I wished I hadn't said anything about the hotel, wished that I had let him surprise me.

"I-I didn't really know," I said falteringly. "Brad said something the other day about your wanting to work there." I hadn't even wanted to think about Brad when I was with Matt, but there was no helping it that time.

"Of course. He would have known. I

should have thought of that." Then he smiled down at me, and I felt little quivers in my stomach.

"He didn't say what kind of job, though. What will you be doing?"

"Bellhopping. I started yesterday. Oh, Jenny," he said, his words coming out in a rush. "I love it. The people. You wouldn't believe the people I've met already. That's why I wanted to work there. I love people. I could have taken a job on an assembly line, staring at a piece of machinery all day, but I would have hated it. I want to be around people."

I had to laugh at his eagerness. "I can believe it," I said, amusement in my voice. "And they get all types at the hotel. Young— old—pretty—" I suddenly wondered how many pretty girls he had met and would meet in the future. I knew some would be prettier than I was, and I felt a little pang of jealousy.

"And they're all so interesting," continued Matt, not noticing my hesitation. "Even the small ones. There was a little girl, Faye, a beautiful kid with long silky hair." He picked up the ends of my hair, which had fallen across my shoulder and rubbed them gently between his fingers.

"She was traveling with her parents and trying to act so grown up, but she couldn't help peering into every room we passed. By the time we reached their room, she was almost dancing with excitement. She reminded me of you."

"Thank you," I said, wondering which part about the little girl reminded him of me, but I could tell from the look in his eyes that it was a compliment.

"And then there was an old couple celebrating their fiftieth wedding anniversary. His name was Henry, and hers was Virginia. They're from Cincinnati, and they have three children, five grandchildren, and four great-grandchildren."

"What did they have for breakfast?" I asked, teasing him.

Matt grinned a little self-consciously and then laughed. "You caught me, didn't you? I guess I get carried away sometimes. But people fascinate me."

"They do me, too," I said, remembering some of the interesting people I'd met at the Retirement Center when I'd gone with Mom.

Suddenly I had an idea. "Maybe you should be a writer, Matt. You seem to have a knack for getting people to talk, to tell their stories, and everyone has a story to tell."

Matt looked thoughtful and then shook his head slowly from side to side. "I don't think so, Jenny. I love to hear the stories, but I don't have the patience to write them down, even if I could find the right words. Writers have to spend so much time alone, and I don't think I'm cut out for that. Now Brad—yes, Brad could be a writer."

I sat up with a start at the mention of Brad's name. Then I remembered his interview with the *Times-Mail* editor. "What about his job on the newspaper? Did he get it?" I asked.

"Yes. I knew he would. When Brad really wants something, he usually gets it. He can be very convincing when he wants to be. He's very intense, you know."

There was a note of pride in his voice, and I was reminded again of how close they were.

"You wouldn't believe where he is tonight," Matt continued. "I asked him if he wanted to come with us, but he said he had other things to do."

"Let me guess," I said, closing my eyes. "The library is open till ten—"

Matt smiled admiringly at me. "You must be a clairvoyant. You're getting to know him, all right. Now me, I prefer going to a movie with a pretty girl."

I laughed and commented, "Brad doesn't

seem too interested in girls. Did he have a girlfriend in Ohio?"

"No. No one special, that is. Brad's like me in that respect. He's very particular." He paused and then added, "I have a feeling that when he does fall, it will be for someone like you."

I hadn't expected him to say that. If Brad had fallen for me, would he let me know or just bow out in favor of his twin?

"What?" I asked, startled by something else Matt had said.

"Want some popcorn?" he repeated. "I had planned to get some before the movie started, but I guess I got too carried away. First by my job and then by you."

"No. Thanks. We had a late dinner." I got the words out, but my voice sounded a little hollow.

"Maybe at intermission, then," said Matt, turning his attention to the screen. Apparently he hadn't noticed any change in my voice.

"Are we going to stay for both movies since we haven't seen them?" I asked later, sounding more like my old self.

"If you want to. You don't have to baby-sit on Saturday, do you?" I shook my head. "And I don't have to go to work until four o'clock," he went on, "so we can stay out as late as we want."

"Except for my curfew," I reminded him. I had to be home by one o'clock.

"Right. The curfew."

"Let's stay," I decided. "The second show will be over by midnight."

Our grandfather clock in the front hall was striking one when I opened the front door. The last chime had hardly faded away before the phone began to ring. With a sinking heart I ran to the kitchen. Phones ringing late at night usually meant bad news.

"Hello," I said, feeling my stomach begin to quiver.

"Jenny?"

I hadn't realized I had been holding my breath until I exhaled with a deep sigh of relief.

"Jenny? Is that you?"

"Elaine!" I said, getting my breath back. "Do you know what time it is?"

"Sure," she replied. "It's eleven o'clock—or thereabouts."

"Eleven o'clock in California. One o'clock in Indiana. Or thereabouts," I added dryly.

"Uh-oh. I goofed, didn't I?"

"Slightly," I retorted. "Wait just a sec." I

laid the phone down, and crossing the kitchen on tiptoes, I closed the door. "There," I said when I picked up the phone again. "That's better. I wanted to close the door so my voice wouldn't wake up Mom and Dad. "Now, what is so important that you had to call at this hour?"

"Your letter. I loved it."

"My letter?" I had forgotten all about the long letter I had written to Elaine, the letter where I told her all about Matt and Brad.

"Yes. Don't tell me you made it all up. There really is a Matt and a Brad, isn't there? If there isn't, I'll never forgive you."

"Yes," I said, smiling at Elaine's threat. "There really is a Matt and a Brad. In fact," I added, "you almost missed me. Matt just brought me home from a movie."

"Did Brad go, too? Were you out with both of them again?"

"No. Only that one time at the hotel."

"I loved that part of your letter, when you went to the spa with the two of them. This is all so romantic! I can't believe it's happening to you, Jenny."

"Neither can I," I said honestly. "What have you been doing with yourself, anyhow?"

"Oh, nothing. Bo-o-oring." I heard a ho-hum yawn, and then Elaine went on. "We just got back from a dull week in L.A. That's why I didn't get your letter until today. I wasn't here when it arrived, and after I'd read it I just had to call you."

"I could have waited for a letter. It would have been a lot cheaper," I remarked.

"Oh, but I couldn't! This is just too exciting! Just imagine, two great-looking guys all to yourself. You wrote about Matt a little more than about Brad, but I've got the feeling that you like both of them."

Keen, perceptive Elaine. "Well—"

"I knew it. I just knew it! Well, you can't have both. You're going to have to give up one of them, and whichever one it is, save him for me."

"You'll have to get in line," I said, laughing. "Sally and Julie have already got their eyes on them."

"Well, do your best."

I told her I would, but I didn't say which one I'd try to "save" for her.

I don't really like to talk on the phone. I'd rather talk to someone face to face so I can see his or her expression and get some feedback from it. There was a lot I wanted to tell Elaine. Besides being a good friend, she's a sounding board for me. Whenever I have a problem, I take it to her, and she helps me solve it. But I didn't want to try to tell her my problem on the phone. Phones are too impersonal, and what I had to say was very personal, indeed.

If she had been there and had asked me if I loved Matt, I would have said, "I think so." For I did love his easy charm and quick wit. And if she had asked me if I loved Brad, I would have had to say "I think so" to that, too. Brad's intensity and mysteriousness were just as attractive as Matt's liveliness. That was the problem.

Chapter Nine

I must have been awfully tired when I finally got to bed because I fell into a dreamless sleep immediately and didn't wake up until Mom called me.

"I'm going to the mall to shop this morning, Jenny," she said when I strolled into the kitchen for breakfast. "Want to go with me?"

"Sure," I said, pouring myself a glass of orange juice. "If you've got time to wait for me to get dressed, that is."

"I'll wait. I can finish my list while you get ready."

"I'll hurry," I promised. I stuck a piece of bread in the toaster and reached for the peanut butter. My favorite breakfast. Mom sipped her coffee while I munched on my toast.

"We can leave the dishes until we get

back," she said. "You know, Jenny, we really ought to be thinking about what clothes you'll need to start back to school."

I could only groan because my mouth was stuck together with peanut butter. After I had swallowed, I said, "Surely it's not time for that already."

Mom smiled fondly at me. "It's getting close."

"Where has the summer gone?" I said more to myself than to Mom. Actually I knew why the past couple of weeks had rushed by. It was because of Matt and Brad.

"Are you and Dad going out tonight?" I asked.

"I think so. Why? Is Matt coming over?"

"No. He has to work. He's on the second shift. I think I'll look for a book or two while we're shopping. It'll give me something to do tonight. There. Finished." I set my plate, knife, and glass in the sink. "Be ready in a jif."

We went to one of the big department stores, and I picked out a couple of pairs of jeans and two new tops. While they were being rung up and wrapped, I wandered over to the dresses and pulled one out. It was off-white with a high lace neck, cinched waist, and full skirt. I held it up to me in front of the mirror. It had a mysterious, romantic quality to it.

Because of its old-fashioned look, it reminded me of Brad. I could picture myself wearing the dress, floating across a dance floor in his arms, my hair swirling down my back.

"It's lovely, Jenny," said Mom, coming up behind me. "Did you have somewhere special to wear it? A dance?"

"No, nowhere special," I murmured, hanging the dress on a nearby hook and sorting through another rack.

"Maybe I should have asked 'someone special'?" There was a twinkle in Mom's eye, and I knew she thought I was thinking about Matt.

I just shrugged and smiled. I knew Matt would have liked that dress, too, though.

"I like to see you in dresses," said Mom. She looked around at some of the clothing displays nearby. "I'm going to poke through the rack over there." She stepped away to the next department while I continued to scan the rack in front of me.

I found a yellow sun dress with big, patch pockets and a square neck on an end-of-summer sale. Perfect for a bright sunny day, I thought. It was the kind of dress that made me feel lighthearted and cheerful. I put the dress aside for further consideration.

A red sleeve caught my eye on another rack, and I separated the dresses to get a better look at it. At first I thought it was just a long blouse. Then I saw there was a black miniskirt attached to it. The skirt was caught up so high under the blouse that it almost disappeared. *Now that's cute, kind of sporty,* I thought. *It'd look great with my black boots and a wide black belt.*

I was holding it up to me, picturing how it would look with my boots and a belt, when Mom came back with another outfit.

"I thought you were looking for something dressy," she said. "That's pretty sporty looking."

"Yes, but I like it. For the right place, that is. Like an informal, but no-jeans, dance?"

"Yeah, it does. And it looks like you, one side of you, anyway." Then she placed the outfit she was holding in front of me and said, "What do you think of this?"

I looked in the mirror and regarded the suit that Mom held up. It was made of pale peach lightweight wool, and it was coordinated with a darker peach-colored silk blouse. The jacket, with its softly rounded lines, ended a few inches below the skirt's waistband.

"I like it," I said. "It would be perfect for dinners out."

Mom smiled, glad that I had approved of

her choice. "Shall we take one of them? Which do you like best?"

I looked again at the dresses that had really interested me—the Victorian lace, the sun dress, the red and black miniskirt outfit, the peach suit—and I shook my head in amazement.

I had picked out four different outfits. I mean really different, as if they were for four different girls.

But I was only one girl. One girl, I suddenly realized, with a wide range of interests, one girl with many sides to her, one girl who was more than just a jeans and sweat shirt girl—or even a dreamy-eyed, romantic girl. All the dresses could fit my personality, depending on my mood.

I hesitated so long that Mom said, "We can't afford all of them, Jenny. Not unless you've saved a lot more money this summer than I think you have."

"I haven't," I told her regretfully. "Besides, right now I'm in a jeans and sweat shirt mood. And it's a good thing because I don't think I could pick a favorite. Let's wait until something comes along that I need a new outfit for. Then it won't be so hard to choose."

We hung all of the dresses back up. And as

the last one fell into place, I thought, *I really am several girls all rolled into one*.

"Mom," I said as we left the dress department, "I want to go to the bookstore. Do you have some other shopping to do?"

"Yes. How about meeting me at the coffee shop in—" Mom looked at her watch—"forty-five minutes? Will that give you enough time?"

"Sure. I could find a couple hundred books in that much time."

"Well, don't buy the place out," Mom cautioned jokingly.

My first stop was in the teen romance section. I found two new books by my favorite author and quickly stuck them under my arm while I picked up another to leaf through.

I wasn't really seeing the pages, though. I was still seeing the dresses and was remembering how each one had appealed to a different side of my personality. I hadn't wanted to choose one dress over the other, and I didn't want to choose one boy over the other, either. Subconsciously I knew I was being drawn more and more to Brad, but I didn't want to lose Matt's very special kind of friendship.

Mrs. Carlton finished her schoolwork, so I had my days free for the rest of the summer, which really wasn't all that long. Still, it left me with a lot of time on my hands, so I was glad I'd picked up those books when Mom and I had gone shopping.

I spent most of my first free day reading, and once again the hero was so like Brad that it was amazing. Brad with his mysterious, romantic air. Matt could be romantic, too, I reminded myself. But he wasn't intense and deep as Brad was.

It was a little after ten that night when Mom called down from her bedroom, "We're going to turn in now, Jenny. Don't forget to lock the doors. And don't stay up all night reading."

"I won't, Mom," I called back from the living room. "But I want to finish this book. I've only a couple of chapters to go."

After Mom closed her door, I riffled through the remaining pages and frowned. The story was interesting, but something just wasn't right. And when I finished it, I felt a little let down. The boy was as good-looking and nice as ever right up to the end, but he just didn't seem right for the girl in the story. She was very outgoing. The boy was too quiet and restrained for her. Oh, well, I thought, maybe it just wasn't very good writing. Maybe the next one would be better.

I laid the book down, locked the doors, and was headed for my room when the phone rang.

"Hello." I got to it before it rang a second time.

"Jenny?"

"Matt!" I was surprised at first and then a little alarmed. It wasn't like him to call so late, and besides, he should have been at work. "Where are you?" I asked. "Is anything wrong?"

"No. Nothing's wrong. I'm at the hotel. Things were slow, and I wanted to ask you something. How would you and your furry friend like to go on a picnic?"

"My fur—? Baffin!" I laughed softly so I wouldn't disturb Mom and Dad. "At this hour?"

"No, no. Tomorrow morning. Glen, a guy who works here, was telling me tonight about some places on the river, and I thought you and Baffin would like it."

"I know the places on the river well, and we'd love it," I said enthusiastically. "But what about your job? Don't you have to work tomorrow?"

"Yes. But I thought that if we left about eight and took lunch with us, we could be

101

back about three. That would give me plenty of time to get to work."

"Sounds like fun," I agreed. "I'll pack a lunch."

"Just sandwiches. I'll bring a cooler and some Cokes. Got to go. Hope I didn't wake you," he added.

"No, you didn't. See you tomorrow."

When I went to bed, I thought about the picnic and how like Matt it was to refer to Baffin as my furry friend. But when I fell asleep, I dreamed about waltzing across a dance floor, in a beautiful Victorian dress, with Brad's arms around me.

Chapter Ten

The next morning, I told Baffin that we were going to the river, and it seemed as though he understood. He trotted excitedly back and forth between the kitchen and the front door while I made the sandwiches. When I finally opened the front door for Matt, Baffin shot out in a flash and headed straight toward Matt's car. He would have jumped in if the door had been open. Instead, he halted abruptly, looked back at us, and barked.

"Wow!" said Matt, looking a little stunned. "I thought he'd like coming with us, but I didn't expect this. It's a good thing I included him in on this outing."

"He'd never forgive you if you hadn't," I said.

I gave Matt directions, and in a little over

an hour we turned off the main highway and followed a narrow dirt road. On one side of us was a cornfield. On the other, often hidden by thick underbrush and tall, white-barked sycamores, was the river.

We were headed for one of my favorite spots, a sandy bar that reached right out into the water. I used to go there quite often, either with my folks or with some kids, but I hadn't been there all summer. I wouldn't ever take Tina and Anne, even if Mrs. Carlton had approved, because the current was pretty strong once you got away from the shore.

Matt parked as far off the road as he could, on the river side. As soon as I opened the car door, Baffin bolted out, took the grassy bank in one giant leap, and scrambled in the water before Matt could even get out of the car.

"It doesn't look like anyone's been here all summer," observed Matt. Tall weeds stuck up through thick, long, tangled blades of grass, covering the steep bank and ending at a narrow stretch of sandy shore. "The least Baffin could have done is make a path for us."

"He's probably halfway across the river by now," I said as I picked up the sandwiches and towels.

Matt went first, carrying the cooler and a

blanket and trampling the taller weeds down with his feet.

"He's all the way across," he said when we reached the sandy shore. "Look at him."

Baffin had gotten out of the water and was on the opposite side about a quarter of a mile away, looking back at us. He gave three short barks.

I cupped my hands around my mouth and yelled, "We see you. Now come back over here." Baffin jumped back in and swam toward us, his head held high.

When he reached our side, he stopped at the edge of the water and shook himself, sending sprays in all directions. Then he trotted over to Matt.

"Good boy," said Matt, patting Baffin on the head and laughing.

"Show-off, you mean. You could have waited for us, couldn't you?" I was speaking to Baffin, but he ignored me.

We had worn our swimsuits. After we set everything in a small, sandy depression, we waded out until the water was up to our waists. We were in a backwater area, a cove. The water was still and almost warm, but I knew that the farther out we went, the colder it would get.

"There isn't much current, is there?" remarked Matt.

"There is if you get out in the middle," I told him. "If we aren't careful, the current will carry us downriver in a hurry. That's kind of fun, but fighting your way back is something else."

I shuddered, remembering a time when I had drifted downriver so far that the cove was out of sight. I had tried to swim back but couldn't make it. By the time I realized I wasn't making any progress, that I was staying in the same spot, I was exhausted. There was nothing I could do except drift even farther downstream, working my way gradually to the shore.

Then I had had a long walk back through the underbrush. It hadn't been one of my better days, and I wasn't too eager to repeat the experience. It had been a little frightening and had given me a healthy respect for the river and its current.

Matt wasn't so hesitant. After we had swum around for a while, he said, "I think I'll go across."

"I'll watch," I said. I walked out of the water, spread the blanket on the sand, then sat down.

Baffin followed Matt across, and when

they reached the other side, they both climbed out and turned around. Matt waved, and Baffin barked.

I cupped my hands around my mouth again and yelled, "Show-offs!"

The river was too shallow along the edges for diving, so they waded back in and started the return trip side by side. Then they reached the shore, they were both a little out of breath.

Matt flopped down beside me and rested his arms on his bent knees. "You weren't kidding about that current, were you?"

"I never kid about things like that," I said solemnly. "I've learned to respect the river." Then I told him about my experience. "Of course, I didn't have Baffin with me," I added lightly. "If I had, he probably could have pulled me back up."

At the sound of his name, Baffin crawled over and put his head in my lap. I leaned down and hugged him.

"Hey, I would have, too. So how about me?" asked Matt with a twinkle in his eye.

"Didn't I just hear you complaining about the current?" I asked. "Think you could have fought it and pulled me along at the same time?"

"Ah, but I would have tried, Jenny."

107

He smiled at me so tenderly that my heart skipped a beat.

"Yes," I murmured. "I know you would have." Neither of us said anything else for several minutes. We just sat there holding hands and gazing across the slowly moving river. Finally he raised my hand to his lips, and my heart turned completely over.

"It must be time to eat," I said, breaking the spell and nodding at Baffin, who was nosing around the sack of sandwiches.

Matt jumped up to move the sack away from Baffin. "I hope you brought some extras. If swimming makes him as hungry as it does me, we're in for a day of fasting."

"I made plenty," I said, laughing and standing up. "Also some Baffin biscuits. He doesn't like them as well as fries, but in an emergency, they'll do."

After we ate, we stretched out, facing the river. An occasional boat went by, but most of the time it was so quiet that I could hear the buzz of a lazy fly and the soft swish of waves lapping the underbrush. I took a deep breath of the clean, fresh air and closed my eyes. The sun, so warm on my back, relaxed me, and I almost fell asleep.

Some time later I was aware of a small

motor not too far away but didn't pay any attention to it until Matt spoke.

"Isn't that your friend?"

"Who?" I asked, lifting my head and squinting out toward the river. The sun was so bright that I had a hard time keeping my eyes open. But I could make out a small motorboat heading toward us. Someone was waving.

"You know. The girl we met on our first date. Melissa, I think her name is," said Matt, waving back.

"Yes," I said, sitting up and shading my eyes. "It is Melissa. Melissa and Guy."

Matt got to his feet and pulled me up with him.

"Hi," Melissa called. "What are you doing?"

"Picnicking," said Matt and I at the same time. Then we both burst out laughing.

Baffin raised his head and regarded our visitors with curiosity. When Guy ran the small boat up as close as he could and cut the engine, Baffin waded into the water.

Melissa stepped out into the shallow water and walked toward us. She glanced around at our blanket and cooler. She looked really fantastic in a pink bikini.

"Want to go for a ride?" she asked pleasantly.

"There's plenty of room," added Guy, indicating a narrow seat in the front of the boat, just wide enough for two.

Matt and I looked at each other. I didn't want to, but I thought he might. It wasn't that I didn't like Melissa and Guy. I just didn't want to share Matt with anyone, at least not right then.

So I was relieved when he said, "I think we'd better not. I don't think there's enough room for Baffin, too, and we have to head back pretty soon, anyhow."

Melissa turned and eyed my dog. "Baffin? Yes, it would get a little crowded with him along. Maybe another time would be better."

Baffin must have thought Melissa was calling him because at that moment he came out of the water, walked over to her, looked up, and then thoroughly shook himself.

"Ooooh!" cried Melissa angrily, wrinkling her nose at the huge black dog. "Could I borrow a towel, please?" I handed one to her, and she dried off the water Baffin had so ungraciously sprayed on her.

Matt grabbed my hand and squeezed it. He kept a straight face, but I knew he was on the verge of laughter.

"Really, Jenny, you should teach that dog some manners," Melissa said, handing me the towel. Then she walked back to the boat, climbed in, and called, "See you around." Guy started the engine, and Matt and I didn't speak until we were sure they were out of earshot.

Then Matt hugged me and we burst out laughing. Finally I got my breath, pulled away, and looked down at Baffin.

"Naughty dog," I said, trying to frown at him.

Baffin cocked his head to one side as if he didn't understand. "You know exactly what I mean," I said with mock severity. "It isn't nice to shake water all over people."

Matt dropped down beside Baffin and ruffled his fur. Then he looked up at me and added, "This has been some day, hasn't it? A very special day. What we need here is something to remember it by." He crawled into the shallow water and began to sift through the sand with his hands.

"What are you looking for?" I asked. "Buried treasure?"

"No. Yes, in a way. Clams."

I knew from experience that there were a lot of freshwater clams there, most of them buried just below the riverbed. I knelt down beside him and started digging, too. Altogether, we found twenty-three shells.

"Have you ever found a pearl in one?" asked Matt.

"I've never even found a clam in one," I replied. "Just empty shells. I wonder what happens to the clam?"

"Fishermen probably use them for bait, and then throw the shells back in the river." He looked at the pile we had collected and sighed. "I wanted to find you a pearl, Jenny."

"I thought pearls were found in oyster shells. Are you sure they're in clams, too?"

"No," said Matt, giving me a disarming smile. "But I was hoping."

We washed the shells and put them in the empty sandwich bag. Then we gathered up our things and headed for the car. I could feel the bag of shells against my foot on the way home and hear an occasional clink when we went around a curve. I knew I would treasure them as much as I would have a pearl. Matt's digging them up for me was the most special part of a very special day with a very special friend.

Chapter Eleven

"Jenny," called Mom when I opened the front door, "is that you?"

She sounded so excited that I dropped my towel right there in the hall instead of taking it out and hanging it on the clothesline.

"What is it?" I asked, hurrying into the living room.

"Look!" Mom had been reading the newspaper and she had it folded back to the "Community Happenings" section. "At first I thought it was Matt," she said. "But it's his brother."

"He made it!" I cried, seeing the small picture of Brad as Mom handed the paper to me. I started to sit down on the couch, remembered my wet suit, and switched to the plastic-covered footstool at Mom's feet.

Brad's article was in the "Then and Now" column. It was a comparison of the health spas of the nineteenth century with those of today. Most of it dealt with food and drink. He even described how the spring water smelled and tasted. I could feel myself smiling as I read that part and remembered the afternoon when I had taken Matt and him on the grand tour. I was proud to have been a part of it.

At the end of the column Brad said that his next article would cover physical activities, and once more, I could see him peering through the pavilion window watching the bowlers as Matt and I chased the salamander.

"He did a good job on it, didn't he?" Mom remarked.

"Yes," I said. "It's very well written." Brad's writing flowed and had a great deal of wit and charm. He had taken a few pieces of historical fact and made them entertaining as well as informative.

"It doesn't sound like the usual essay from a sixteen- or seventeen-year-old," mused Mom as I reread the item.

That's because Brad isn't the usual seventeen-year-old, I thought. On the surface he appeared to be a shy, quiet version of his more outgoing brother. But inside he was a fascinating mixture of confidence, intelligence, warmth, compassion, and wonder. I had glimpsed parts of Brad's true self at the spa and at the library and pool.

His writing revealed still another facet of his personality. There was nothing shy or reserved about that newspaper article. Nothing was held back. It showed me that Brad was an extremely talented but complicated person. There were many sides to him, just as there were many sides to me. Maybe that was why I felt myself drawn to him.

Matt usually had his nights off during the week when there weren't so many people checking in and out, so I wasn't expecting to see him the following Friday or Saturday night. I was both surprised and delighted when he called me that Thursday afternoon.

"How about Friday night, Jenny? Want to go to the drive-in? I think I can swap shifts with one of the other guys."

This time I knew what was playing. It was a movie we had talked about and both wanted to see. "I'd love it," I told him. "If you're sure your bosses won't mind."

"They don't care if we swap shifts, just so long as we tell them. I'll let you know as soon as I get it set up."

When we hung up, I got out the old power

lawnmower, and after four strong pulls on the cord, I finally got it started. The grass was pretty high, so it took a little more time and a lot more effort than usual. I was worn out when I finished, so I took a long, hot shower. Then I flopped down on my bed, just for a short rest, I told myself. But my short rest turned out to be almost two hours of solid sleep.

I'm always hungry when I wake up, even from a nap, so I headed for the kitchen for a snack. That's when I found the note from Mom, saying that Mrs. Carlton was trying to get hold of me. Mom must have thought I'd gone somewhere after mowing the lawn while all the time I was upstairs asleep. I postponed my snack long enough to phone.

"Oh, Jenny, I'm so glad you called," said Mrs. Carlton. "Can you baby-sit tomorrow night?"

That was Friday, the night Matt was going to try to get off work. I paused too long.

"You have something planned, don't you?" Mrs. Carlton asked, her voice filled with disappointment.

"Well, it's not definite," I said, hedging.

"George got a promotion, and his boss wants to take us out to dinner. We won't be gone very long," she added, a pleading note in her voice.

I hated to say no. They went out so seldom, and besides, I thought I could get hold of Matt and tell him to ask for Saturday night instead of Friday.

"Sure," I said. "What time?"

"Seven. We should be back by nine-thirty or ten. And thanks, Jenny. This means a lot to us."

I called Matt's house as soon as she hung up, but there was no answer. Then I realized he would already be at work, and I decided to call him there.

"May I speak to Matt Hunter, please?" I asked when a pleasant-voiced woman answered the phone.

"Is this a personal call?" asked the receptionist.

"Yes."

The tone of her voice changed immediately. "Employees are not permitted to accept personal calls. Only emergencies." She sounded like a recording. I thanked her and hung up. It was an emergency, in a way, but not one I thought the impersonal voice would understand.

I hoped Matt wouldn't find anyone to

switch with, but he did. It wasn't half an hour later that the phone rang.

"We're on, Jenny," said Matt. "Joe was looking for someone to work for him next Tuesday so he could go to his parents' anniversary dinner. It worked out perfectly for both of us."

"Oh, Matt," I said, unable to keep my frustration from showing. "I tried to reach you earlier, but they wouldn't put me through. Mrs. Carlton asked me to sit tomorrow night, and I told her I would. I thought we could change our date to Saturday night. Do you think Joe would change back with you?"

There was a long pause, and I knew Matt was as disappointed as I was. "He can't, Jenny. He works Saturday night himself. Look," he said, sounding a little more cheerful, "we can go to the movie some other night. It's not all that important. And we can still see each other. They won't be out very late, will they? Why don't you give me a call when they get back, and I'll come over to your house."

"I'll do that," I said, relieved that he wasn't angry, but then I should have known he wouldn't be.

I was on my way out the door that next night when Mom called me to the phone.

"It's Mrs. Carlton," she said. "You aren't late, are you?"

"No," I replied, taking the phone from her and wondering what Mrs. Carlton wanted me to pick up for her.

"Oh, Jenny, I'm so sorry," began Mrs. Carlton.

"That's OK," I said. "What do we need? Milk? Bread?"

"Oh, no, dear, nothing like that. It's Tina. She has a dreadful fever, and I don't think I should leave her. She came down with it just this afternoon. George wanted to go out, anyway. He said she'd be perfectly all right with you and we could leave a number for you to call if you needed us. And I know she would, but I just don't feel right, leaving her and all. I'm so awfully sorry. I know you had something planned, and now it's too late for you to go ahead."

She ran her sentences together, probably because she felt guilty, I thought. I tried to reassure her that it was all right.

"It's OK, Mrs. Carlton. I understand. I just hope Tina's fever breaks pretty soon and that it isn't anything serious."

"I think it's just a twenty-four-hour virus. But she's feeling so bad right now that I hate to leave her."

"It's OK," I repeated a little more firmly. "I'll call and check on her tomorrow."

There was still plenty of time to get to the movie, so as soon as Mrs. Carlton hung up, I dialed Matt's number. His mother answered.

"Is Matt there?" I asked.

"No," she said and then, "Jenny?"

"Yes."

"Matt said you'd be calling, but he thought it would be much later. I'm afraid he isn't here, and I don't know where he went. But he did say he'd be home by ten."

With a sinking heart I thanked her, hung up, and sat down at the kitchen table with my chin in my hands.

"Plans awry?" asked Mom sympathetically.

I nodded. "You got it." Then I shook myself and sat up a little straighter. *No use sitting here all night,* I thought. *I might as well do something, go somewhere, since I'm dressed and everything. At least for a couple of hours. Maybe Matt will be home by then.*

I decided to drive out to the mall. I might run into some of the gang.

I spent over an hour in the bookstore, just browsing, not buying. Then I window-shopped, wondering where everyone was. When I came to the shop where Jody worked, I pushed open the door and went in.

She looked up at the sound of the door chime and grinned. "Jenny! What brings you down this way?"

"I was just wandering around, saw you in here, and decided to drop in." I leaned both elbows on the countertop and propped my head on my fists.

"Hey," said Jody, narrowing her eyes and peering closely at me, "you look like you just lost your last friend, but I know you haven't because I'm still here. So what's wrong?"

"Nothing."

"No one looks like you do over 'nothing.' So give! Is it the twins?"

I straightened up, grinned at Jody, and shook off my light case of the blues. It wasn't like me to mope, anyhow, and just grinning made me feel better.

"It really isn't anything, Jody, at least nothing serious." Then I told her about the mix-up. "I think I'm just more bored than anything else. You're the first person I've seen tonight who looked even halfway familiar."

"I think everyone went to the movie here tonight. That's where Bill, Melissa, and Guy are. They're going to meet me here when it's over."

"Bill?" I asked, wondering why he hadn't waited until Jody could go with him.

"We went last night," explained Jody, reading my mind. "It was the only night I had off this week. Bill liked the movie so much he decided to go again."

The door chime sounded as two ladies came in. "Got to go," whispered Jody. "Here. Have a look at this." She handed me the magazine she'd been looking at, put on her best smile, and went to help her customers.

I pulled a high stool out from behind the counter, sat down, and flipped open the magazine, which turned out to be a Christmas catalog.

"They're just looking," said Jody a few seconds later. "Almost everyone is tonight. Things have really been slow. Mrs. Webster asked me to look at some of the gifts in that catalog and give her a younger person's opinion." Mrs. Webster was the owner of the shop.

"Isn't it awfully early to be thinking about Christmas?" I asked.

"Not when you have to order things. She's already bought decorations, so skip that section and go to the toys."

"Toys?" I asked. "Good heavens, Jody, you're not that young. What do you know about toys anymore?"

"Nothing really, but neither does Mrs. Webster. Do you remember how we used to get together and have parties for our Barbie dolls? I still have mine," she added sheepishly.

"So do I," I admitted, leaning forward so that the two ladies wouldn't overhear. My Barbie dolls were carefully tucked away in a box on the top shelf of my closet. They were about the only things from my childhood that I hadn't been able to part with yet.

"Remember when I made a ball gown for one of my dolls?" I began to giggle as I recalled the dress.

"Do I?" asked Jody, shaking with laughter. "It looked like something Cinderella wore *before* she met her fairy godmother. It was dreadful."

"Well, after all," I said, feigning indignation, "I was only seven years old. And, as I recall, you didn't do too good a job on yours, either."

"Ugh," said Jody, grimacing. "I'm still not very good with a needle and thread. Now cooking is something else. Remember when . . ."

We did a lot of remembering in the next half hour. I laughed so hard that my sides hurt. Jody, Elaine, Melissa, and I had done some pretty crazy things together in all the years we had been friends. I kept trying to top Jody's stories with sillier ones of my own.

"Stop it!" cried Jody, wiping tears from

her eyes. They were tears of laughter, but there was also a wistful expression on her face, and I knew she was feeling a little sentimental, as I was.

"We've got to get down to business now. How do you like this doll?" Jody pointed to a newer Barbie version, one with a western outfit, and I studied it carefully.

We looked at several more dolls, and voiced our opinions on which ones we thought would sell the best. Then we discussed the merits of everything from toy tractors to toy space shuttles.

I was having such a good time that I didn't realize how late it was until Jody looked up from the magazine to peer at the clock on the wall.

"Hey, it's time to close," she said. "I'm locking up by myself tonight."

I slipped my purse straps over my shoulder and waited by the front door while Jody cleared the cash register and turned out the light. While I waited, I saw a few people drift out of the movie, which was just on the opposite side of the mall. Then a few more came out.

"I think the first show's over," I said.

"Good. Timed just right." Jody and I

stepped out into the mall, and she locked the door.

"I'll wait with you," I offered.

"Why don't you come with us?" Jody suggested. "We're just going over to Charlie's. You could call Matt from there."

I considered the idea and then decided against it. It wasn't that I wouldn't be welcome. We often had an extra person when we got together, especially in a place like Charlie's. I guess I just wasn't in the mood for lots of company at the moment.

Chapter Twelve

Bill, Guy, and Melissa arrived a few minutes later. They, too, asked me to join them, but I declined, telling them that Matt and I might drop over later and if they were still there, we'd join them.

After they left, I stopped at one of the food stands, bought a Coke, and was looking for a table when I spotted Brad sitting alone at a small corner table. He was reading a book and hadn't noticed me. I went straight to him, smiled, and asked, "Mind if I join you?"

"Jenny!" His face broke into a dazzling smile, and he stood up and pulled out the chair next to him. "Please do. I thought you had a date with Matt tonight."

"I did. I mean we do," I said. "Later. I was supposed to baby-sit, but that was canceled at the last minute. I tried to call Matt, but he wasn't home. So I decided to come out here for a while."

"I'm glad." When he realized what he'd said, he looked embarrassed and tried to explain. "I mean I'm glad you came out here. I'm sorry you didn't get hold of Matt."

"I'm glad I came out here, too." I sounded like a parrot, and I felt awkward. Here I was alone with him again, and I didn't know what to say. I guess that I was starting to think that Brad was the one for me, and I didn't know how to tell him.

"Hey," I said, remembering his column, "I liked your article. It was great."

"Thanks." Brad's eyes lit up at my praise. "I was doing a little more research when you came in." He held up a small paperback on fitness exercises. "I just bought it at the bookstore tonight and sat down to read for a while. I guess that's why I didn't see you."

I could understand that. Brad was just like me in that respect. When I get wrapped up in a book, I don't know what's going on around me, either. "Is that for your next article?"

"Yes. I covered food and drink in the first one, you know, and promised to compare physical activities in the next one. Actually, there's not all that much difference except where the girls are concerned. I found an old pamphlet in the library describing a gentleman's day at the old spa, and guess what?"

I pretended to be thinking real hard and finally said, "I give. What?"

"There was a gym on the ground floor—near the kitchen—with weights, rings, horses—"

"Horses?" I asked, teasing him. "Inside?"

He laughed. He was so different when he was really enthused about something. "Not the four-legged kind. The padded kind, the kind you vault over."

"Did you find anything for the girls to do except loll around waiting for the men to come around?"

"Not yet, but I'll keep on looking. That's where most of the fun is anyhow. Doing the research. Like that day in the library." He smiled shyly again, just as he had then, and my pulse raced. "It's sort of like a puzzle," he went on. "A mystery waiting to be solved."

"And once you solved it, what then?" I asked.

"Then it's on to the next one. The past is fascinating, Jenny, not only because of what happened but also in the way it affects us today. Do you realize that if it hadn't been for

Augustus Lystrom, this town wouldn't even be here? That was a good lead you gave me."

"I thought it might help," I said. "I know he was one of our founding fathers."

"Not one, Jenny. The. If it hadn't been for him you might be living in—Alaska!"

"And you might still be living in Ohio," I said, caught up by his enthusiasm. And we would never have met." I felt a chill come over me and almost shivered. "But aren't you exaggerating a little?"

"No." He shook his head emphatically. "Listen." Brad scooted his chair over a little and leaned closer to me, his face glowing. "Old Augustus came from the next county. He was a born gambler and a good one, too. He started out by just working in a gambling house over in Sharpsville, but by the time he was eighteen, he owned it."

Brad went on to give me a brief rundown on how Augustus built his fortune, his hotel, and his town. "So you see, Jenny, this whole area would probably still be a cornfield if it weren't for him."

His expression changed suddenly from eagerness to concern. He sounded almost apologetic when he added, "I guess it's hard to understand. Most people think I'm some kind of a nut for spending so much time on something that happened a hundred years ago. I'm probably boring you."

"No, you're not," I insisted. "I think it's very interesting. And it's something I should have known, myself." But a little voice inside told me that these facts weren't really important to me.

Then I thought back to what Brad had said about puzzles and mysteries. He had been a puzzle and mystery to me, but now I was beginning to understand what motivated him.

"The people you described in your article are very real to you, aren't they?" I asked. "They'd have to be for you to make them come alive on paper."

"Sometimes more real than real people," said Brad ruefully. "Or maybe I should say they're easier to get to know than real people. I just don't relate to people very easily—not at all like you and Matt. It's like two separate worlds—the one I live in and the one you and Matt live in.

"Oh, I'm not complaining. I like my world. I feel very much at home in it. More so than I do in your world." He wasn't feeling sorry for himself, just stating what he thought was the truth.

And I realized, then, that Brad wasn't a

mystery at all. He was simply a very private, intense person, not one who could open up easily to other people. He was more comfortable spending long hours alone researching history than he was interacting with kids his own age. That was fine for him, but it wasn't for me. Brad's revelation made me realize that in real life I preferred someone quite different, someone more open and lively, someone like Matt.

I tried to reassure him by leaning forward, placing my hand on his arm and saying, "You reach far more people than Matt or I ever could. You do it through your writing. So, in a way, your world is much broader than ours. You . . ."

The words died in my throat as I glanced up and saw Matt strolling toward our table. He was still quite a bit away, but he was looking right at us. I quickly removed my hand from Brad's arm, wondering if Matt had seen the intimate gesture.

Chapter Thirteen

Matt's face broke into a big grin as he got closer to us. If he had seen my hand on Brad's arm, either it hadn't bothered him or he had recognized it for what it was, a friendly, concerned gesture. I shouldn't even have given it a thought. Matt had probably known from the beginning that he was the one for me.

"Two of my favorite people," he said, pulling a chair over from another table and straddling it.

"You and Jenny got your signals crossed tonight, didn't you, Matt?" asked Brad. He ran the "you and Jenny" together, and it almost sounded as if we were one person. As if we belonged together. We did, and it sent another chill down my spine, a chill of excitement, and this time I did shiver.

"Cold?" asked Matt.

"Not now," I said meaningfully.

"What happened, Jenny? I went home about an hour ago, and Mom said you'd called. I tried your house, but no one was home, so I called the Carltons'. Mrs. Carlton said they'd decided not to go out."

"Tina got sick. I didn't know about it until I was almost ready to go over there. If I had I would have called earlier."

"I probably wouldn't have been home then, either, unless it was a lot earlier. I spent most of the afternoon playing softball. Brent has really been hounding me, and I thought it would be a good chance since I had the day off and you'd be busy until pretty late."

"How did you find me?" I asked.

"I said to myself, 'Now what would I do if I were Jenny? She doesn't have any plans because she was saving the evening for me. Now, what does my Jenny like to do? Well, she likes to read, but she'd do that at home, and since she isn't there, she isn't reading. So, what else does my Jenny like? She likes people. And where are there more people than anywhere else? The mall!'"

He finished with a proud smile. "My deductive abilities didn't fail me, did they?"

"No," I said happily because he had called

me 'my Jenny' and had been able to think like me. But why shouldn't he have been able to? We were on the same wavelength.

I thought about how close I had come to spoiling it all, and my stomach did a quick flip-flop. How could I ever have thought Brad was the one for me? Had I gotten him mixed up with the heroes of my books? He was like them in many ways—strong, silent, confident, but was that what I really wanted? No, what I wanted was someone like Matt.

Brad would always be very dear to me, but it was Matt who could charm and delight me.

"I did make a little side trip past Charlie's," Matt admitted, "but I didn't go in. I'd already been by your house and saw that both cars were gone, so I figured you had one of them. And I know you usually walk over to Charlie's."

"Charlie's!" I cried with a start. "I ran into some of my friends out here, and they asked us to join them there. Want to?"

"Maybe. Later."

"Why don't you come with us, Brad? Where did he go?" I hadn't heard Brad get up, but he was gone. Then I noticed that almost everyone was gone except us.

Matt stood up, a frown creasing his forehead. "He wouldn't have left without telling us." Then his frown disappeared. "Here he comes."

I looked over my shoulder and saw Brad heading our way. He was carrying three Cokes, holding them in a triangle with his fingertips touching.

"Made it. Didn't spill a drop," he said, setting the paper cups down in front of us. "I was going to ask you first if you wanted anything, but you were lost to the world." He smiled fondly at us. "Bet you didn't even miss me."

"We did," Matt said firmly. "Didn't we, Jenny?"

"Yes," I said as the two boys sat back down. "I was about to ask you if you'd like to go to Charlie's with us."

"Thanks, but no. I've got work to do." He patted the little paperback book.

Matt looked at the title and groaned. "More research?"

"Yes. I've found some fascinating bits in the library, and I needed some backup information. I was telling Jenny about it when you came in."

"Is that why she looked so happy to see me? Was it because you were boring her?" There was too much mischief in his voice for him to have been serious.

"I don't think that was it," said Brad, looking as mischievous as his twin.

"It was really interesting, Matt," I said. Then I turned to Brad and asked, "Why don't you tell Matt what you found out about old Augustus."

We sat there sipping our Cokes while Brad talked. Matt was a good listener and asked some very pointed questions, questions that proved he was not only listening, but was interested as well.

"Hey," I said a little later. "They're turning off the lights. I guess we'd better go." We threw the remains of our sodas away and started down the long, deserted corridor. Our voices echoed, bouncing off the ceiling and the store fronts.

Since you aren't going with us," suggested Matt, "why don't you take our car, and I'll go with Jenny."

"Suits me fine," said Brad. "Where did you park?"

"On the east side."

"I'm on the south," I said. "So I guess we'll have to split up here."

Matt and I stood there shoulder to shoulder and watched Brad walk toward the other exit. Before he rounded the corner, he turned to us and waved. He looked very alone, but I knew he wasn't lonely. He had too many things to think about for that. And someday he'd also have a girl to think about. But it wouldn't be me.

"Let's go." Matt took my hand and led me through the south door and across the parking lot, where I handed him my key. Neither of us said anything until we were seated side by side in the car. Then Matt turned to me.

"Did you promise we'd show up at Charlie's?" he asked.

"No, I just said we might drop by."

"Do you think they'd mind if we didn't?"

"No, of course not."

"It is pretty late—"

"And they might have left by now."

"Should we just forget it?"

"Let's!"

"I'd much rather talk, Jenny, just you and me." He took my chin in his hand, tilted my face up, and looked into my eyes. "There's so much I want to say to you." He brushed his lips softly across mine before letting me go. "And I know just the place for it," he said as he started the car.

I sank back against the seat with a happy sigh as he pulled out of the parking lot and turned toward the old spa. There was a lot I wanted to say to him, too.

We hope you enjoyed reading this book. All the titles currently available in the Sweet Dreams series are listed on page two. They are all available at your local bookshop or newsagent, though should you find any difficulty in obtaining the books you would like, you can order direct from the publisher, at the address below. Also, if you would like to know more about the series, or would simply like to tell us what you think of the series, write to:

Kim Prior,
Sweet Dreams,
Transworld Publishers Limited,
61–63 Uxbridge Road,
Ealing, London W5 5SA.

To order books, please list the title(s) you would like, and send together with your name and address, and a cheque or postal order made payable to TRANSWORLD PUBLISHERS LIMITED. Please allow cost of book(s) plus 20p for the first book and 10p for each additional book for postage and packing.

(The above applies to readers in the UK and Ireland only.)

If you live in Australia or New Zealand, and would like more information about the series, please write to:

Sally Porter,
Sweet Dreams
Corgi & Bantam Books,
26 Harley Crescent,
Condell Park,
N.S.W. 2200,
Australia.

Kiri Martin
Sweet Dreams
c/o Corgi & Bantam Books
  New Zealand,
Cnr. Moselle and Waipareira
  Avenues,
Henderson,
Auckland,
New Zealand.